American Horse Tales

The Dust Bowl

by Michelle Jabès Corpora

Penguin Workshop

To my parents, Mania & Angelino, who gave me faith;

To my husband, Adam, who gave me passion;

To everyone at 88, who gave me courage;

And to my daughters, Gwen & Ellie, who reminded

me never to give up on a dream—MJC

W

PENGUIN WORKSHOP

An Imprint of Penguin Random House LLC, New York

Copyright © 2021 by Penguin Random House LLC. All rights reserved. Published by Penguin Workshop, an imprint of Penguin Random House LLC, New York. PENGUIN and PENGUIN WORKSHOP are trademarks of Penguin Books Ltd, and the W colophon is a registered trademark of Penguin Random House LLC. Printed in the USA.

Visit us online at www.penguinrandomhouse.com.

Library of Congress Control Number: 2021932445

ISBN 9780593225257   10 9 8 7 6 5 4 3 2 1

Chapter 1
A Nice Day for a Ride

Keyes, Oklahoma
July 1936

I stood out by the barn, the paint peeling off it like an old snakeskin. Closing my eyes, I took a deep, deep breath. Most days, the air was chock-full of dust, but that afternoon it was real clear. Full of nothing but sunlight and the smell of Ma's Ivory Snow laundry soap. I smiled.

"Ready, boy?" I asked, a leather lead in my hand.

At the other end of the lead, my horse, Thimble, looked over at me. He was light gray with jet black stockings, but since he ain't hardly ever got a wash, the dust made him look tarnished, like an old spoon. Sometimes I wondered if we all don't look that color. Once that red dust gets into you, it's real hard to get out.

I'd already checked Thimble's hooves, eyeballed the tack, and tightened the saddle straps around his belly. He nickered, a soft rumble in his throat. *"That's a silly question, Ginny,"* he seemed to be saying. *"I'm always ready!"*

It must have been two weeks since my last ride. Between going to school whenever the weather wasn't too bad and Ma keeping me busy doing odd jobs around the farm, I barely had time to do more than give Thimble his oats and hay. But not that day. I'd slipped away before Ma could make me do the sweeping like she always did after church on Sundays. As soon as I climbed up onto Thimble's saddle, all my troubles just melted away. Up there, under the huge, unbroken sky, I finally felt like I was free.

Seemed like I wasn't the only one fixing to run, either. As soon as Thimble reached the open plain outside the farm, he tore into a gallop, kicking up great clouds of dust that hung in the air behind us like a parade of ghosts.

The dust was everywhere those days. It crept under the front door, filled up Pa's work boots, and slipped between our bedsheets at night. Sometimes it even found its way into my breakfast bowl of mush. If I wasn't so hungry every morning, I'd probably spit it out whenever some of that grit got in. But usually, I just added a little more sugar and tried not to think about it too much.

When I was little, there weren't no dust at all. Back then, Oklahoma was green as green. The corn stood at attention like soldiers in the field, sweet and yellow and as tall as Pa. A cool breeze would blow through the husks when the sun went down, making a sound like *shhh, shhh*. But when the rain stopped falling, the corn all turned brown—and when the wind turned hot and mean, the corn got too tired to stand up anymore. That's just how it looked as Thimble and I rode past: laid low on the dusty ground, as quiet and still as a graveyard. It felt like the whole world was holding its breath, and the only sound was Thimble's hooves thundering across the earth.

"Whoa, Thimble," I said after a few minutes. "Can't go too far from home now—or we'll miss supper." Thimble slowed to a canter and then to an easy jog. "Good boy," I said, combing my fingers through his mane, which was as thick and black as Pa's.

I'd had Thimble for five years, but it might as well be forever. I still remember Pa telling me that the Atwoods' old mare, Hannah, had foaled, and that they weren't sure what to do with the colt because he was so runty. They used their horses to work the fields and didn't think the wobbly little thing could manage it. I begged Pa to buy him, said I would make sure he came to good use on our farm. Ma said the money would be better spent on fabric to make a dress that wasn't torn in three places, but I pulled out my prettiest please so Pa couldn't help but give in.

As soon as I laid eyes on him at the Atwoods' farm, it was love, pure and simple. He ran over to the gate the moment I came up, like he already knew I'd come just for him. But it was what happened on our way back that was really special. I was walking alongside him on the path when all of a sudden, he pulled on the reins, stopping me in my tracks just as something long and dirt-colored slithered across the way. I'd almost stepped on a rattlesnake! "He's like a little thimble, that one," Pa had said, giving my new horse a pat. "Not much to look at, but seems like he'll do a good job keeping you from harm."

The name stuck. Thimble never did grow to be very big, but that didn't matter much. If I asked him to pull the whole world on a cart for me, I'm pretty sure he'd go ahead and do it.

As we rode along the fence line toward the edge of our land, Thimble took a deep breath and sighed, as if he were saying, *"Ahhh . . . What a nice day for a ride!"*

I smiled. "It is nice, ain't it?" It was still hot but not too bad, and any little break in the scorching heat wave we'd been having felt like paradise. The sky was a blue marble with wispy clouds that didn't hurry by, but hung around to give us a little shade here and there. "One day," I said dreamily, "when the rain comes back, all this will be green again. And you and me can work the land together. What do you think of that, boy?"

Thimble whinnied. I think he agreed that this was a good day for dreaming.

As a matter of fact, that day was the first in a long while that everybody in my family was feeling top dollar. When I got out of bed in the morning, I found Ma humming the gospel and opening every window in the house to let the fresh air blow in. We'd all put on our Sunday best, even me. Now, I'd much rather be in a pair of overalls than a dress, but Ma made me put one on, anyway. My sister, Gloria, was thrilled. She put on her fanciest frock and flounced around the kitchen like she was the queen of England. Ma says that when I'm sixteen, I'll want to be just like Gloria, but I reckon that's just Ma's wishful thinking. She's never really known what to do with me. Pa, on the other hand, took to teaching me all the things that boys know, on account of him never having a son. And let me tell you—it ain't easy doing all those things in some fancy dress.

We all strolled out to church with the neighbors, everyone smiling and talking like things were normal again. Still, pretending things were normal was hard, even on good days. The church pews got emptier by the week, with so many families moving to California, where there wasn't any dust and jobs were ripe for the picking.

"We ain't going," I'd heard Pa say to one of the other farmers after the sermon was done. "Things are bad," he said. "But they ain't *that* bad. Not yet at least." I was glad. Even though life in Keyes was no picnic, it was home. I couldn't imagine having to pack up and leave. Pa always told me that our blood was in this land, ever since my great-grandfather bought it, back at the turn of the century. He farmed it, my grandpa and my pa farmed it, and one day I planned to farm it, too. I once told Pa that I was going to take over when he was too old to do it himself anymore, and he laughed. But I wasn't joking. I was deadly serious. So tell me: How was I supposed to do that if we sold it all and went to California?

Pushing all those worries from my mind, I tried to concentrate on enjoying the ride. "Speaking of picnics," I said to Thimble after a while, "you know what I'd like to eat, if I could have whatever I wanted?" His ears swiveled back, listening. "I reckon I'd have a plate of Ma's fresh biscuits just drowning in some sausage gravy. And, for dessert, a big slice of pecan pie, all to myself."

Thimble nickered. *"What about me?"*

I laughed and scratched behind his ears. "Don't worry, boy, I wouldn't forget about you. How about a basket of fresh apples with a few sugar cubes on top? Wouldn't that just be heaven?"

I expected Thimble to nicker again, because there's nothing my horse loves more than a handful of sugar cubes, but he didn't. Instead he slowed to a stop, his body suddenly as tense as a guitar string. He raised his head high and opened his dark eyes so wide, I could see the whites all around them.

"What is it?" I asked. I'd been so caught up with thoughts of rain and California and hot buttered biscuits that I hadn't noticed how cold it had gotten. I hadn't bothered changing out of my blue gingham church dress to ride, which would probably make Ma bawl me out once I got back. I had been plenty warm in it all day, but I got to shivering as a chill wind started to blow in my direction.

By then, Thimble was really fretting something serious. He pawed the ground, drawing long, jagged lines in the dust, and he took a few steps back toward home. *"Something's wrong,"* he seemed to be saying. *"Very, very wrong."*

I raised a hand to my forehead to block the glare and looked around, searching for whatever had got Thimble so spooked. Our corner of Oklahoma was as flat as a pancake, so from just about anywhere, you could see for a hundred miles or more across the high plains. I looked past the neighbors' old farm, past the huddled roofs of downtown Boise City, and then—I saw it.

A great black cloud the size of a mountain was sat right there on the horizon. But unlike the mountains in my schoolbooks, this one was moving—turning and twisting in on itself like a living thing that was darker than midnight and bigger than creation.

It was a dust storm. A whopper. And it was headed straight for us.

"Go, Thimble! Go home!" I shouted, my heart already galloping in my chest.

Thimble whinnied in reply and made a tight turn before breaking into a run so fast, it had me holding onto his saddle for dear life. All around us, the air crackled, alive, electric, and getting dustier by the minute. I pulled out the red bandanna I kept in my saddlebag and held it over my face as we crossed back onto our land. The ride seemed to pass in an instant, and before I knew it, I was throwing myself out of the saddle, tying Thimble's lead to the gate, and dashing into my white clapboard house, with the scraggly bushes out front and the porch that sagged a little to the left.

I burst through the door, startling everyone

sitting at the kitchen table. The house looked spick and span after the morning's cleaning, and the windows were all still wide open.

Pa was ladling out bowls of soup at the head of the table while Ma passed around a basket of cornbread to the neighbors who had come to eat. Gloria sat in her chair, her church dress somehow still clean and pressed even after a whole day of wearing it. She looked up at me, judgment in her eyes, as I banged in like a billy goat.

"Virginia Mae Huggins!" Ma said, standing up with her hands on her hips. "What in the world has gotten into you, comin' into the house like that? You are almost thirteen years old, you should know better! Where you been?"

"Close all them windows, quick!" I yelled, breathless. "There's a duster comin'! A big one!"

Ma's expression went from mad to scared in a

snap. "Another duster?" she asked, her eyes turning to the sky outside. It was a question we seemed to ask all the time. Even though the storms came as regular as Sunday mass, we still kept on being surprised every time they did.

A moment later, the bright sunlight streaming through the kitchen windows started to fade. And then a low moan filled the air, like some angry spirit had come to haunt us. That sound got everyone moving. Everybody scrambled to shut the windows and stuff towels and sheets into the cracks. I moved to help, too, but then I remembered: Thimble was still out there.

"I've got to get Thimble into the barn before the storm hits!" I shouted over the noise and turned back to the front door.

"Ginny, no!" Pa called out. "It's too dangerous!"

"Don't you even *think* 'bout goin' out there,

young lady!" Ma commanded, starting to make her way toward me.

"I can't jus' leave him!" I cried and threw open the door, shutting it and my parents' protests out behind me.

Outside, I could see the duster coming up the edge of our land, a wall of darkness like something from a nightmare. Stuff from the farm was blowing around like crazy. Old newspapers, Ma's little flower pots, and half-filled sacks of corn all tore past the porch like tumbleweeds. I grabbed a pair of goggles from the shelf and put them on to protect my eyes, then dunked my bandanna in a bucket of water before tying it tightly around my face. *Okay, boy,* I thought. *I'm comin' for ya.* But when I looked at the hitching post where I'd left Thimble, all I could see was the rope he'd been tied to whipping in the wind.

My breath caught in my chest. He must have

gotten scared and bolted. I wanted to shout for him, but the roaring storm would only steal my words away and fill my mouth with dust.

Thimble, I thought, my heart racing. *Where are you?*

Chapter 2
The Black Blizzard

I ran out into the front yard, nearly catching my death on the rusty old plow that lay half buried in the dust. The blowing wind was pushing and shoving like a bully on the playground, but somehow I stayed on my feet. I peered into the cornfields and over at the neighbors' farm across the way, but my horse was nowhere to be seen. And it was getting harder and harder to see anything at all, with the storm coming up through the gate like an uninvited guest. Behind me the sun still shone on a bright afternoon, but beyond the duster, it was as black as night.

I was running out of time.

Flying specks of grit stung my arms and legs as I ran around the side of the house. I thought Thimble might have gone to his favorite spot out back, where the buffalo grass used to grow. I heard a screeching sound and looked up to see the squeaky windmill spinning so fast I thought it might just take off like an airplane. I hurried to where the sunburned grass stood in sad little patches, but Thimble wasn't there, either. A lump rose in my throat. *If he ain't here,* I thought, *he could be anywhere. And I don't have time for anywhere.*

"Thimble!" I shouted through the damp bandanna, so worried that I didn't even care how much dust I might breathe in. I sounded no louder than a field mouse against the roar of the storm, but out of the corner of my eye, I saw a twitch of movement. I turned to squint at the little garden shed nearby and saw a black tail flick behind it.

There!

I dashed to the shed, and sure enough, Thimble was hunkered down behind it, taking shelter from the wind. Thank goodness I'd found him! I reached for his bridle to lead him to the barn where we'd be safe, but I must have looked a fright with my goggles, bandanna, and my hair flying every which way, because as soon as he laid eyes on me, he squealed, jumping away in terror.

"Whoa, Thimble, whoa!" I said, yanking the bandanna down off my mouth and pushing the goggles up onto my forehead so he could see my face. "It's me, see? It's Ginny!"

Thimble's ears swiveled toward the sound of my voice, and I could see his body relax a little. He whinnied, like he was saying, *"Oh, it's you!"*

I went to grab his bridle again, and this time he let me do it. Pulling my goggles and bandanna back on, I clicked my tongue to get him to follow me toward the barn on the other side of the house.

But before I could take two steps, the duster hit. Hard.

I felt my body get blown back by the thick, choking dust all around us. Everything went dark, like somebody had thrown a gunnysack over my head. I couldn't see my own hand in front of my face, no less the barn up ahead. But there was nothing for it. We had to keep going or else we were going to die out there. We were pointed in the right direction, so I just had to hope that we didn't get turned around along the way. I took a step forward, pulling Thimble's lead with me. I might have worried that he'd get to fussing again, but my horse always finds his courage when it comes to protecting me from harm. He started to walk, one hoof in front of the other.

I slung an arm over Thimble's neck as we inched forward, counting the steps as we went.

One, two, three . . .

The storm whipped my skin raw and tore at my dress, but we kept walking.

Eight, nine, ten . . .

It took nineteen steps for us to reach the barn, but it might as well have been a thousand. By the time I reached the barn door, I felt like I'd been rubbed all over with sandpaper. Thimble's head hung low, his eyes squeezed shut and his breathing shallow. But at least we'd made it! The storm was still going strong, though, and the gathering dust was so deep that it was almost up to my knees. I needed to get us inside before we both got buried in it. I grabbed the iron ring on the door and pulled—but the wind was blowing so hard that I couldn't get it open.

I pulled and pulled, but every time I got the door open a crack, the buffeting wind slammed it shut again. "Ugh!" I screamed, hitting the door with my fist. "Open!"

I was fixing to punch a hole straight through that door when a hand came out of the darkness, taking hold of that iron ring with me. Even though it was as dark as midnight, I'd recognize that big, leathery hand anywhere.

Pa!

I turned to see my father appear out of the gloom, blown in like an angel without wings. He was wearing his own goggles and blue bandanna over his face, and his black hair and beard were coated with dust. Pa wasn't a big man, but Ma always liked to say that he had a big spirit, and I knew that stubborn barn door didn't have a chance against his strength.

Pa gave me a nod. *Ready?*

I tightened my grip on the iron ring and nodded back. *Ready.*

Together, we heaved at the barn door. My muscles screamed as I pulled with all my might. *C'mon, c'mon!* I thought, my heart thumping in my ears. Finally, the door flew open, hitting the wall of the barn with a terrific bang.

Yes!

I ran inside, pulling Thimble along with me. Pa tumbled in after us, shutting the door and the bellowing storm out behind him.

The first thing I did was rip the goggles and bandanna off my face and cough up a heap of dust. My throat was scorching. I ran over to the little trough and scooped out handfuls of water to drink and splash onto my face. By the time I stood up again, I could see that Thimble had walked up to have a long drink, too.

I reached over to stroke his neck. "Good boy," I said softly. "We're okay now."

I heard a *skritch!* and turned to see my father lighting a match, touching the flame to a few candle nubs we kept lying around the barn. Pa carried one over to me, and in the warm yellow light of the candle, I could see that he'd taken off his goggles and bandanna, too.

I almost wished he'd kept them on, because I could see, plain as day, that Pa was spitting mad.

"D'you have *any* idea how dangerous that was?" he shouted. "What were you thinkin', runnin' out in the storm like that?"

"I-I was just thinkin' about Thimble," I stammered. "He coulda died out there."

"You *both* coulda died out there!" he said. "He's

only a horse, Ginny—*you're* my girl! You can't jus' do whatever you want, whenever you wanta do it." He crossed his arms. "Maybe your ma's right. Maybe I been lettin' you run wild for too long."

"But see," I said, opening my arms wide. "Everything turned out jus' fine! You're fine, Thimble's fine, I'm fine ... This dress might need to be put out to pasture, but other than that—"

"Ginny, this ain't no time for wisecracks. This is serious."

I swallowed, my throat stinging. Even through all the hard years—when the corn crops failed, when we had to sell the cattle, when Ma had to start making clothes out of flour sacks—Pa always managed to go on with a smile and a twinkle in his eye. This was different. And I didn't like it one bit.

"Pa, I'm awful sorry," I said. "But listen, I—"

"Naw, Ginny, you listen," he interrupted, his

voice low. "Your ma and I are tryin' our darnedest to keep this farm goin' and this family strong. Now, I know we ain't perfect, but we are tryin' our very best."

Pa sighed, a sound that seemed to go straight down into his bones. "If we're goin' to make it through it all," he finally said, "you can't be actin' like this, Ginny. You jus' can't. I got so much to worry 'bout round here—I can't be worrying 'bout you, too."

My cheeks burned. If I could have melted into the floor right then, I would have.

Pa's face flickered in the candlelight, the shadows making him look older and tired. "Is that clear?" he finally said.

"Yes, Pa," I answered, looking at the floor.

A silence fell over us then, and together we listened to the duster blow as it passed over, rattling at the barn doors and shutters like a phantom. Pa stood by the window, looking out, his hands on his hips.

I ran my fingers through Thimble's mane, feeling all kinds of things, all of them bad. I felt awful about making Pa so angry, but at the same time, I was angry, too. What was I supposed to do? Just leave Thimble out in the storm? He wasn't *just* a horse— he was my friend. Why couldn't anyone understand that?

As if he knew what I was thinking, Thimble nuzzled me, his velvety nose rubbing the side of my face. I reached back to rub him behind the ears the way he liked it. He nickered softly and leaned against me. I pressed myself against his side and tried to let the feeling of his breathing calm my own.

Suddenly, the storm outside didn't seem so terrible compared to the one in that barn.

Chapter 3
Blown Away

It was a good long while before that duster blew over. When it was finally quiet outside, Pa cracked the barn door open and peeked his nose out, sniffing the air like our old farm dogs used to do.

"Looks like we can rest easy now," he said, his voice cracked and dry. "Storm's done."

"What time is it?" I asked, standing to brush some grit off my dress. I'd taken a seat on a hay bale that Thimble was nibbling on. He tossed his head and huffed loudly through his nose when I got up, like he was saying, *"Time to go? Thank goodness!"* I reckon my horse didn't like being cooped up any more than I did.

Pa opened the door wider and peered outside, the setting sun lighting up his face with an orange glow. "Prob'ly sometime after seven o'clock," he muttered. "Still got a bit of light left." He propped the doors open, and I blinked into the sudden brightness. I followed him outside, Thimble trailing behind me.

"Well," Pa said, as he stopped to survey the land. "Ain't that a thing to see."

I gasped as I finally got a good look at what the duster had done to our poor farm. It was bad, real bad. Everything that had been set outside was strewn all over the place, bent, beaten up, or just plain broken. There was nothing left of the veggie garden Ma had planted. All the little tomato plants and cabbages she'd nursed from seeds were gone. But what the storm had taken wasn't as bad as what it had left behind: Rolling hills of red dust covered everything as far as I could see, ankle deep out in the cornfields, waist deep in the drifts. It was like we'd been transported to the desert or maybe even another planet.

"Ma's garden . . . ," I said. I picked up one of the little wood sticks she'd used to mark where the seeds were planted. She'd written POTATOES on it in fancy letters, like putting that in the ground might magic them into growing, even without any rain. I gripped the little stick in my fist until it hurt. Thimble knocked his head into mine, like he knew I was fit to bust and he was trying to calm me down. I rubbed his snout and sighed. I had every right to be mad, but the problem was, there weren't nobody to be mad at. I guess I could just be mad at the whole world for the drought, the dusters, the heat, and everything else—but what good would that do?

"Brush off a bit and head on inside, Ginny," Pa called out. "Your ma is prob'ly out of her mind with worry by now, so don't let's keep her waiting no more."

I nodded and followed Pa to the front of the house, tying Thimble back up to the hitching post. Before I went inside, I filled up his nosebag with plenty of oats and fitted it on his head. "I'll be back later," I whispered. He flicked an ear at me and tucked into his meal.

When we walked into the kitchen, Ma was sitting at the supper table, her head in her hands. Her blonde hair tumbled down her shoulders like a silken waterfall, making her look beautiful and sad. I touched my own blonde hair and thought that I must look like something the cat dragged in.

Hearing the door open, Ma looked up and said, "Oh my gracious, you're alive!" She ran toward us, and at first, I wasn't sure if she was going to hug me or hit me, but in the end she just grabbed me by the shoulders and said, "Don't you ever scare me like that again!" Then she turned to Pa. "I hope you've talked to her, Joe, 'cause you know that girl won't listen to *me*!"

Pa's mouth was a hard line. "I talked to her, Lina," he said. "Don't you worry none about that." He glanced at me with a look that could fry an egg. I gulped.

Ma tried to smooth my wild hair but quickly gave up and sighed. "I'm gonna go take a look out in the yard," she said. "See about cleanin' up some things."

But Pa held her back. "Ain't nothin' gonna change from now till mornin'," he said. "I'm starved, and Sam and Alice been waiting purty long for their supper, too. We oughta get everybody fed 'fore it gets too dark."

Ma nodded and went to help Gloria ladle the soup and pull the biscuits out of the warming drawer. Maybe Pa really did want his supper, but I thought it were more likely that he didn't want Ma to see her poor, blown-away garden just then. The day had started so nice, maybe he just wanted it to end that way, too.

I went to sit next to Gloria at the table. She was the spitting image of Ma—tall and elegant as a willow tree. "You're filthy," she said, wrinkling her nose when I reached to grab a spoon. "Ma's gonna have to hose you down in the yard 'fore you go to bed."

I shook a little extra salt into my bean soup. "Aw c'mon, Glo," I said. "Why you gotta be so mean?

Ain't you glad I'm alive?"

Gloria snorted and took a dainty sip of her soup. "There ain't a duster in America strong enough to blow you away. I weren't worried for a minute. Still, you're filthier than a pig in mud, so I'd 'preciate you keepin' your distance till you get a bath."

I smiled to myself and tucked into my supper, crumbling bits of biscuit into the bowl. I didn't realize how hungry I was until I started to eat.

"Hey, Joe," Mr. Wilson piped up. "Could you turn on WKY? Prob'ly just 'bout time for the news." Sam Wilson and his wife, Alice, lived on the farm next door. They used to grow a dozen or more acres of wheat on their land, along with keeping chickens and a few dairy cows. But since the drought, their luck had run out just like everybody else's.

"Sure thing," Pa replied and walked over to switch on our little Crosley radio.

A few bars of familiar music played until a crisp voice began to speak. "Good evening, ladies and gentlemen," he said. "Here is the eight o'clock news for today—Sunday, July nineteenth, nineteen thirty-six."

We all ate in silence as the man on the radio said all the things we were so used to hearing:

"Millions of Americans are still out of work, even as the economy improves—"

"A record-breaking heat wave continues to scorch the nation—"

"No end in sight to the historic drought hitting the Great Plains, as savage dust storms destroy farms and homes across the region—"

Click.

I looked up to see Pa at the radio, his weathered hand on the dial. Instead of the newsman, soft piano music started to play. "Not really in the mood for the news, after all," Pa explained. Everyone nodded in understanding and turned back to their soup.

A lady's voice, thick and rich, spilled from the speaker. *"I wished on the moon,"* she sang, *"for something I never knew, wished on the moon, for more than I ever knew . . ."*

The song made my heart hurt, though I couldn't quite figure out why.

When supper was done, I helped Gloria wash and dry the dishes, and we all said our good nights to the Wilsons. It was full dark outside then, and quiet except for the rhythmic chirping of the crickets. I went to my bedroom to change, and I was brushing the dust from my hair when I overheard Ma and Pa talking in the next room.

"I know how much this land means to you," Ma was saying, "but we got to think 'bout our family, 'bout our girls. We got nothin' left here, Joe. You keep sayin' that next year's gonna get better, but how long can we keep waitin'? My cousins got a nice little place in the valley in California, and they say there might be a job there for you. I could start doin' some sewing work again, and—"

"We're not goin'," Pa broke in, his words as heavy and unmovable as stone. "We got three generations on this land, and I ain't fixing to be the one to leave it behind. I'll get one of them WPA jobs buildin' roads and bridges, and we'll jus' have to tighten our belts for a while till this weather breaks and we can get a good crop growin' again."

"Our belts are plenty tight already, Joe," Ma argued. "What we got left to sell, anyway?"

Pa didn't answer right away. And in the quiet of that moment, a fright took hold of me, like I knew something terrible was about to happen.

"We can sell Ginny's horse," Pa finally said.

I gasped, his words like a punch to the gut.

No!

"Feedin' and carin' for 'im ain't cheap," he went on. "And I bet I could get a purty good deal for 'im in town. He's a fine beast, after all."

"I s'pose we could sell 'im," Ma said carefully. "Guess I'm surprised to hear you say it. You're always the one tellin' her to ride and—"

"Things change," Pa replied coldly. "Can't afford to be sentimental when we got to worry about gettin' food on the table. I'll talk to Ginny now. She'll hear sense."

I was sitting at my vanity mirror when Pa came into the room behind me. We locked eyes in the reflection, and right away I could tell he knew that I'd heard everything. "You can't," I said, my voice breaking. "You jus' can't."

"I'm awful sorry, Gin," Pa said. He was looking

at me, but somehow it seemed like he was far away. "But this here's the way it's gotta be." He squeezed my shoulder once, gave me a kiss on the top of my head, and then walked out.

It wasn't until I ran outside and buried my face in Thimble's mane that I let myself cry.

Chapter 4
Not for Sale

I must have made it back to my bed sometime that night because the next thing I knew, I was waking up to the sound of Ma rattling around in the kitchen. I slipped out of my room to see her piling all kinds of things on the kitchen table: a white ceramic vase, a glass cake plate, and the teacups with the pink roses inside. "Ma, what're you doin'?" I asked.

Ma looked over and flashed a quick smile that didn't reach her eyes. "Oh, jus' puttin' some stuff together for your pa to sell in town," she said. "Don't need these things no more."

I picked up one of the delicate white teacups. Ma had always kept them in a secret place in the cupboard, only taking them out for special occasions. "But I thought you loved these," I said. "Didn't Nana give 'em to ya when you and Pa got married?"

Ma gently took the teacup back and placed it with the others. "S'okay, Ginny," she said softly. "It's not important." With that, she turned around and kept sifting through the cupboards, studying each item she found there.

I looked down at the teacups, clustered together like a pile of abandoned puppies. How could she just sell them off like they meant nothing? A hot anger rose in my cheeks. When Ma wasn't looking, I swiped one off the table and hid it under my bed.

A few minutes later, Pa walked in from outside,

kicking the dust from his boots at the door. "I got the truck loaded up with all the extra equipment I could spare," he said to Ma. "Gloria's out takin' care of the chickens. That duster left the coop in a right mess, so I tol' her to do her best cleanin' it out. I'm headin' up to Boise City now 'fore the heat sets in."

"Wait, you ain't taking Thimble today, are ya?" I asked, my heart starting to race.

Pa's nostrils flared, and he looked at the floor. "I got to, Ginny. Better to get it over and done with— waitin' is only gonna make it worse. I'm sure I'll find him a nice new home."

At first, I wanted to scream and pound the floor, but I knew that wasn't going to do me no good. I could see from the set of Pa's jaw that his mind was made up. But pretty soon I got a better idea, an idea that just might keep Thimble home with me a little longer. "Okay, Pa," I said softly. "But how 'bout I come along with you to town?"

Pa looked surprised, like he was expecting me to start a fight. "I don't think that's a good idea," he said. "Ma could use your help cleanin' up round here."

"How you gonna get Thimble into town without a rider?" I asked. "You tie him to the truck and try to lead him, he'll spook. He don't like bein' so close to all that noise."

Pa blinked. I just stood there with my hands clasped behind my back, as sweet and pure as a church choir on Sunday. Finally, he put his hands on his hips and sighed. "Fine," he said. "You can ride him into town. But I don't want no funny business, y'hear?"

I nodded and ran to get dressed.

After pulling on my overalls and getting Thimble fed, watered, and saddled, I was ready for our ten-mile journey to Boise City. Pa got into the old truck, which had taken him all morning to clean off, and I hoisted myself up onto Thimble's back, and we were off. Truth be told, if we had been going for any other reason, I would have been excited. But as it was, the hunk of cornbread that Ma had given me to eat was sitting in my stomach like a brick, heavy with worry. Thimble seemed to know something was wrong. His body was tense, and his ears swiveled constantly, listening to the sounds of cars and people that only got louder as we rode into town. I reached into my pocket and felt for the sugar cubes I'd swiped from the kitchen before we left. They were kinda mushy from the heat but not too bad. I needed them if the plan I'd cooked up was ever going to work.

We passed the Palace Theater, where Pa had taken Gloria and me to see *Treasure Island* a couple of years back as a special treat. Gloria thought it was loud and scary, but Pa and I loved it. I'd read our old copy of the book so many times that the pages were falling out, and it was something special seeing Long John Silver himself up on that screen. The place looked a little worse for wear—I guessed there weren't many folks left who could still afford to pay for a ticket.

I followed Pa's truck to a big lot where a bunch of other loaded-down trucks were parked. Men in dusty overalls were talking to other men in dark suits, who I guessed were the buyers. Pa pulled up to an empty spot, and I rode up next to him. While Pa went to speak to one of the buyers, I jumped down from the saddle and whispered in Thimble's ear. "When those men come over here," I said, showing him the sugar cubes in my pocket, "jus' keep your eyes on me and do what I tell you, okay?"

Now I know folks would say that a horse couldn't

really understand what I was saying, but I swear that when Thimble looked at me with those big, dark eyes, he knew. He pawed the dusty ground as if to say, *"I'm ready. Let's do this."*

A minute later, Pa came over with four buyers who started picking over our things like a bunch of buzzards. After they were done with the stuff in the truck, they made their way over to Thimble and me. "We also got this quarter horse to sell," Pa was saying. "He's kinda small, but he's in real good shape. Strong, too. Ain't never thrown nobody, either."

One of the buyers, a shiny-faced man with slicked-back hair and jowls like a bulldog, came over to inspect Thimble. He didn't pay me no mind, which was exactly what I wanted.

"He's got good teeth," the buyer said, pulling at Thimble's muzzle to get a look inside. My gentle horse didn't bite him—though part of me wished he would. "An' a shiny coat, too. Not bad. He fit for work?"

"Sure is," Pa said, looking hopeful. "He's a fine, hard worker."

I felt sick. *This is it,* I thought. *It's now or never.* I clicked softly with my tongue, and Thimble instantly looked my way. I smiled, feeling a little bit hopeful myself. Because there was something that neither the buyers nor my pa knew: Thimble had a few tricks up his sleeve.

When the buyer took up Thimble's lead to make him walk, I pointed at Thimble's hoof. Following the command, Thimble raised his foreleg off the ground and hobbled forward on three legs. "What's he doin'?" the buyer asked, his eyebrows furrowing.

"Um, I dunno," Pa said, alarmed. "Ain't nothing wrong with his leg . . ."

"You sure about that, fella?" the buyer asked.

He sounded very suspicious.

One of the other buyers, a thin, sour-faced man with a handlebar mustache, came around and gave Thimble's flank a slap. "Go on now," he barked. "Let's see how you go."

In response, I softly clicked again and pointed down. Thimble pulled back on his bridle with a stubborn neigh and dropped to the ground. "What's wrong with him?" the first buyer said, looking at Thimble lying there. The buyer with the mustache tugged on Thimble's lead, but my horse didn't budge. "Is he lame, stubborn, or what?"

Pa was sweating. He looked at me for an explanation, but I just shrugged. "I swear, that horse is in perfect health, maybe he's got a rock in his shoe or somethin'. Please, if you'd jus'—"

But the buyer men seemed like they'd already made up their minds. "We'll take all them bits and bobs in the truck for ten dollars, but you can keep your horse."

I let out the breath I'd been holding in a great sigh of relief. We'd done it! Thimble was safe!

Pa wasn't nearly as pleased. "Ten dollars?" he exclaimed. "But there's good-quality equipment in there! The farm tools alone are worth at least fifty."

The buyer shrugged. "Take it or leave it," he said. "Your choice."

Pa took the cap from his head and used it to wipe the sweat from his brow. The sun was beating down hard on us, and I was perishing for a glass of water. "Well?" the buyer asked. "We got other customers to attend to. Better make up your mind while the deal's good."

Pa curled his hands into fists and looked away, toward the horizon. "All right," he said. "Take it."

Fifteen minutes later, after Pa had unloaded

all the stuff from the truck and taken his money, I climbed back up on Thimble's saddle and got ready for the ride home. "Good boy," I murmured in Thimble's ear and sneaked him a handful of sugar cubes. As I followed Pa's truck out of town, I saw him look back at me and hit the brakes.

"Thought he had a hurt leg," Pa said, his head poked out of the truck window.

"Guess he worked it out," I said, trying to sound innocent. "Maybe it was a rock in his shoe, like you said."

But Pa saw right through me. He always told me I could never play poker because I was terrible at bluffing. He got out of the truck. "What did you do?" he asked.

"Nothin'," I said. But I knew the jig was up. If I didn't confess, it would only be worse for me later. "I jus' . . . got Thimble to do a few little tricks," I finally blurted, "so that those awful men wouldn't want 'im."

Pa looked fit to burst. "Virginia Mae," he shouted. "When will you understand that this ain't a game? That horse ain't cheap to feed, and we need that money to stay on the farm! We need it to keep a roof over our heads and food on the table! This is our *life*, Ginny!"

His anger bit into me like a mosquito sting. "What kinda life is it if we get rid of everythin' we love?" I shouted back. "Nana's teacups, the gold necklace Gloria got for her sweet sixteen, and now Thimble!"

"They're just *things*!" he said. "Why can't you see that?"

"Thimble ain't no thing, Pa!" I said, my anger boiling over. "He's my best friend! Why can't you see *that*?"

Pa stomped the dusty ground with his boot. "Darn it, girl—these days are hard enough without you always makin' 'em harder! Sometimes I don't know what to do with you!"

I opened my mouth to shout back at him, but nothing came out. Pa had never said anything that hurt me before, not like that.

"Now, listen here," he went on. "Tomorrow, I'm bringin' that horse back to town, and I'm gonna talk to those men and make 'em understand what you done. And the money I'll save plus what I get from sellin' 'im will keep us afloat for another month or two till we can get the fall crop in. You wanna be mad, fine. But one day, when you're grown, you'll understand why I had to do this." And with that, Pa got back in the truck and started the engine.

At first, I just stared after him, panting, my hands balled into tight fists. When I finally got ahold of myself, I took Thimble's reins, and we followed slowly behind Pa's truck. Every few minutes, Thimble turned back to look at me with big, sad eyes. I felt trapped, stuck between my wanting to keep Thimble and helping my family. "What am I gonna do?" I asked no one in particular.

Just then, we passed an old jalopy packed to the brim with furniture and suitcases, trundling down the highway. There was a little painted sign nailed to the side that read: CALIFORNIA OR BUST!

An idea popped into my head, maybe the craziest idea I'd ever had. "Thimble," I whispered, "what if *we* went to California, jus' you and me?" After all, if Pa couldn't afford to feed Thimble, then I'd bet it would be easier on everyone if he didn't have to feed me, either. Plus, I could track down Ma's cousins over in the valley and maybe get a job picking in the fields. Then I could send all the money I made back home until things got better. Pa needed every nickel and dime he could get to be able to keep our land; he said so himself.

Pa said that I'm always makin' things harder for everybody, anyway. The thought stung, but I ignored it and squared my shoulders. *They'll prob'ly be better off when I'm gone.*

By the time we arrived back home, I'd made up my mind. After everyone was in bed that night, Thimble and I were packing up and heading west.

Chapter 5
Runaway

Ever since I was small, Ma liked to tell people I got three things from my father: his eyes, his laugh, and his bullheaded ways. So when I got the idea to run away to California, it was all I could think about, and nothing—I mean *nothing*—was going to change my mind. I finished up all my chores quick as can be and then spent the afternoon sneaking around the farm, collecting supplies and food for the journey and stashing them in the barn.

Pa didn't say a word to me all day, even at supper. Ma and Gloria, who knew better than to get in the middle of one of our quarrels, steered clear of us both. After I washed my dishes, I went straight to the barn to give Thimble a good grooming. "Say goodbye to this place, boy," I said, going over him with the little round curry comb I used to brush his coat every night. "Tonight, we're goin' on a long trip, and we ain't coming back for a while. Okay?" Thimble whinnied and leaned into the brush like he had an itch I was scratching. Truth was, Thimble and I were always ready for an adventure. And this was going to be the biggest one yet.

Round midnight, long after everyone else was in their beds, I got up and put on my best pair of overalls and a wide-brimmed hat. In the next room, I could hear Gloria snoring like an old engine. She swore up and down that she'd never snored in her life, on account of it not being very ladylike, so hearing it made me chuckle. Made me a little sad, too, but it wasn't the time for all that. It was time to go.

Once I got my boots laced up, I made my way out of the house to the barn, where my stuff was ready and waiting. Thimble was awake and seemed as excited as I was, his tail raised like a flag as I set to fitting him with the pack and his saddle.

That done, I hoisted myself up onto Thimble's back and clicked my tongue to get him moving. "Let's go now," I whispered to him. "Real quiet-like." We walked out past the house and down the front path, and it wasn't until we got to the road that I looked back.

When will I see this place again? I wondered. *The old slouchy porch, the chickens in the henhouse, the Wilsons and the Atwoods, my school friends, Gloria, Ma—*

Pa . . .

A lump started to rise in my throat, but I swallowed it down. Part of me felt downright awful leaving without saying boo, but I knew that if Ma or Pa had any idea what I was up to, they'd stop me. And as soon as the sun rose on tomorrow, one of those buyer men would take Thimble away for good.

No. I couldn't let that happen.

It's like Pa said: This was the way it had to be.

"Goodbye," I said and urged Thimble down the road into the night.

⌒

Thimble and I rode for a few hours across the open highway heading west, only stopping at a little pond for water and in a patchy field so Thimble could take a load off and graze awhile. We saw a couple of trucks and jalopies on the way, but mostly we had the dark road to ourselves. Eventually we passed by a billboard with a picture of a sleeping boy that read: "Next Time, Try the Train! Travel While You Sleep! Southern Pacific." Looking at that boy made me yawn. I was plum tuckered out. "Whoa," I said to Thimble and pulled the reins to steer him behind the billboard. After tying his lead to a post and making sure he had room to lie down, I wrapped myself in an old quilt and settled down on the dirt, resting my head on my pack. The quiet of it all made me feel kinda lonely. So I scooched myself over to where Thimble had set himself and curled up beside him. "It'll be okay, boy," I said quietly. "As long as we stick together. Right?" Thimble just sighed, so I closed my eyes and listened to him breathe.

Some hours later, the glare of the bright morning sun woke me from a dreamless sleep. A skinny jackrabbit was sitting on his haunches just a foot away from where I was lying, watching me with huge black eyes. When I sat up and stretched, he bounded away in a flash, his long ears flattened against his head like he was guilty of something. "Hope you didn't let that rabbit steal none of our stuff," I said to Thimble, who was busy grazing nearby.

Thimble stopped his munching long enough to look at me with his head cocked, like he was saying, "*Rabbit? What rabbit?*" I could hardly blame him— he probably worked up quite an appetite during our ride, so he was far too hungry to care much about some nosy critter.

My stomach growled watching him eat, but I wasn't ready to tuck into my rations too much just yet. I had to make sure I had enough for the whole journey. So I took a swig of water from my canteen and nibbled a piece of leftover fried cornmeal that I'd taken from the kitchen before Thimble and I left.

While I ate, I watched the cars on the highway go by. The road was crowded with them, bristling like porcupines with table legs and tools poking out of their backs, all of them heading west. Sometimes I saw little kids sitting in the truck beds, their clothes, shoes, and faces the color of dust.

I squinted at a sign across the way, which had a road number inside the outline of Texas. We must have crossed over the state line last night! From what I'd seen when I'd studied Pa's map, I just had to stay on this until I hit Route 66, which would take me the rest of the way to California.

I had just rolled up my quilt and finished packing everything up into Thimble's saddlebag when I heard it. A long, low whistle, off to the south. I turned my head toward the sound and saw a finger of gray smoke rising from a locomotive that crawled like a black snake across the horizon.

A steam engine!

Although I'd seen pictures of freight trains in

schoolbooks, I'd never actually seen one with my own eyes. The closest railroad was a whole county away from home, and we'd never had reason to go there. This was my chance! I leaped astride Thimble and urged him into a gallop toward the tracks.

With the wind in my hair, we flew across the scrubby field, scattering half a dozen jackrabbits as we went. I raised myself a few inches off the saddle, keeping rhythm with Thimble's rolling gait. Pretty soon we were close enough to the train to really see it. The engine was as shiny as my church shoes, and had the words ROCK ISLAND painted in white across the coal car behind it. More than a dozen boxcars and flatcars trailed them, lumbering along the tracks with a terrific *chugga-chugga* sound.

We stopped a good twenty feet back and watched it go by, and I held onto my hat to keep it from blowing away. "Lookit that, boy!" I shouted over the noise. "Ain't that a sight!"

But then I saw something else on that train.

A boy. Running across one of the flatcars like Death himself was chasing him.

I squinted as the flatcar got closer. The boy looked probably about my age, and he wore a gray cap and a pair of overalls not unlike mine. A burlap sack was slung over his back, and it bounced as he ran.

Then another figure popped out of the train car behind him, and I saw why he was running.

The man was tall and broad, and he wore a black uniform with a billy club hanging from his belt. He mounted the flat car and caught sight of the boy. "Stop right there!" the man shouted, chasing after him. "You're gonna be sorry when I get my hands on you, you little brat!"

As the flat car sped past where Thimble and I

were standing, I caught sight of the boy's face as he fled toward the front of the train. Our eyes met for an instant. "Help!" he cried out. "Help me!"

Chapter 6
A One-Horse Race

The wind whipped the boy's shouts away as the train thundered by. *Who is that boy?* I wondered. *And why is that man after him?* But I didn't have time to think or to have any of my many questions answered. I had to decide, and fast. Was I going to help or not?

Thing was, it seemed like Thimble had already decided what to do. He pawed the ground, kicking up a cloud of dust, as if to say, *"C'mon, Gin, let's go!"*

"Well," I said, gripping the reins tight. "If you

say so." I clicked my tongue and squeezed Thimble's sides with my heels, and he took off like a rocket.

Something I don't often mention about my horse: He may be small, but he is *fast*.

Thimble galloped beside the tracks, huge clouds of red dust billowing up from his hooves. Bent low into the wind, I squinted ahead to see the boy and the man in black on a flatcar loaded with lumber. I passed the man, who glanced over at me curiously. "Hey!" he yelled. "Get away from there!"

I felt the blood drain from my face—was I doing the right thing? What if I got in trouble? But then the desperation in the boy's eyes came back to me, and I felt that old bullheadedness set in. Maybe that boy had done wrong, but I didn't think he deserved whatever was coming to him.

"Sorry, mister," I shouted back at the man in black. "Gotta run!" I squeezed my heels a bit more, and Thimble put on an extra burst of speed. By then, the boy was standing in between the flatcar and the boxcar in front of it. Thimble was catching up, but he could only run like that for so long. Then I glanced up ahead and got another shock.

The train was coming up to a trestle bridge. On either side of the tracks, the land fell away into a deep gulch, and we were coming to it fast. If we were going to get that boy off the train, we'd have to do it before there was no more ground to run on!

The boy must have seen the look on my face because he peeked around the side of the boxcar himself and paled at what he saw. "Hey, kid!" he shouted at me. "You've gotta hurry or I'm done for!"

"Who're you callin' a kid?" I yelled back. "And can't you see we're comin' as fast as we can?"

The boy shrugged and pointed to a steel ladder that was bolted to the back corner of the boxcar near where he was standing. "I'm gonna climb down there!"

I nodded, and the boy pulled himself onto the rungs. He hung there off the side of the train, the harsh wind buffeting him and blowing his gray cap right off his head and away. I nudged Thimble closer to the train, so close that I could almost reach out and touch it. The muffled *chugga-chugga* became a roar that drowned out everything else.

Sweat was glistening on Thimble's neck as he ran—I could tell he was getting tired. I turned back to see the man in black at the end of the boxcar reaching out for the boy, shouting all kinds of angry words. Ahead, the bridge was almost upon us, and I could see where the ground dropped off to nothing. Looking back at the boy on the ladder, I shouted, "Whatever you're gonna do, you best do it quick!"

The boy looked at me and then the ground flying

past beneath him. "Okay, I'm gonna jump!" he cried. "Keep that horse steady with me!"

'Course I'd known this was his plan from the start, but it was only then that I realized just how crazy it was. "Wait, wait!" I yelled. "This ain't gonna work! You're gonna fall!"

"No, I ain't! Just trust me, all right?"

I don't know why I trusted that boy, but I did. "All right! Go!" I answered.

The boy closed his eyes for an instant, as if to say a prayer, then leaped from the ladder.

He seemed to hang in the air for a moment. I held my breath, gripping the reins so tight that my knuckles were white. And then—

He crashed down across Thimble's back behind me, scrabbling for a handhold. Thimble whinnied and lurched to the left with the extra weight. The boy latched onto the saddle straps but was still slipping, his feet sliding along the ground. "Hold on!" I yelled. Reaching back, I grabbed the boy by the back of his shirt and yanked on him with all my might. From there, he pulled himself up and wrapped his arms around my waist. I could feel his heart hammering as I pulled back on the reins, shouting, "Gee, Thimble! Gee!" Thimble swerved to the right just in time to avoid us tumbling off the gulch's edge into the dry riverbed below. The train thundered past, taking the man in black with it. I caught a glimpse of him peering back at us, his face purple with rage.

And then, he was gone.

I slid from the saddle to the ground, my legs wobbly, and coughed. My lungs had been feeling raw ever since that last duster, and this whole episode with the train hadn't helped one bit. I gave Thimble's neck a pat and pulled an apple from my saddlebag for him to eat. "Good boy," I said as he took it from my hand and crunched it in half.

The boy jumped down, too, and I finally got a good look at him. He had skin like caramel; a wide, broad nose; and a nest of curly brown hair. He brushed the dirt from his overalls, which were too short, and looked back at me with dark eyes that sparkled with mischief. "See?" he said. "What'd I tell you? Piece of cake."

I snorted. "You gotta be kiddin' me. You're lucky you didn't get killed!"

The boy waved my words away like a swarm of flies. "Naw. It'd take more than a bump on the head and one of them fool 'bo chasers to kill me."

"'Bo chaser? You mean that man in black? What'd he want you for, anyway?"

"Oh, they go after anybody tryin' to ride the rails," the boy said with a shrug. "'Specially Mexicanos like me."

I shook my head. There weren't many Mexican folks in Keyes, but I'd seen a sign or two in Boise City about places that wouldn't serve them food or let them buy things. It weren't fair to treat people differently on account of what they looked like. "Well," I said, "I think that's jus' awful."

"Yeah, I reckon it is," he replied. "Anyway, I'm glad you showed up when you did. Jumpin' off a train onto a horse has got to be the most excitin' thing I've done all week." He grinned and stuck out his hand. "Name's Silvio Hernandez," he said, giving me a firm shake. "Nice to meet you. Guess I owe you one."

"I'm Virginia Huggins," I said, "but everyone calls me Ginny." I glanced back to see Thimble munching up the rest of the apple, the juice running down his lips. "You got my horse to thank more than me," I continued. "He's the one who done all the work." I took the little bucket down from where I'd tied it to the saddlebag and poured some water in for Thimble to drink.

Silvio dropped his pack and went over to Thimble, who sniffed him with his wet muzzle. *"Gracias, Señor Caballo,"* he said, wiping the horse slobber from his cheek with a laugh. He turned back to me. "Got to be a purty good horse to outrun a freight train."

"He's good, all right," I agreed. At that moment, my stomach growled—loudly.

"Wow," Silvio said. "Didja swallow a badger or are you jus' hungry?"

I crossed my arms over my stomach. "Guess I haven't really eaten much today . . . ," I admitted, my cheeks getting hot and turning red.

"You're in luck!" Silvio said brightly, grabbing his pack. "I got a feast fit for kings right here." He untied the knot in the sack and began taking things out of the bag: half a loaf of white bread, some bologna sausage, and a big hunk of cheese.

My mouth started to water just looking at it. "Where'd you get all this?" I asked in wonder. Store-bought food was a luxury for most folks nowadays.

"Oh, I did a little work washin' dishes in one of them roadside diners before I hopped the train," Silvio said proudly. "They said they'd pay me in leftover food instead of money, and I was fine with that. C'mon, let's eat!"

"Oh, I can't take your food," I said, shaking my head. "Sounds like you worked hard for it. Wouldn't feel right."

Silvio looked at me with one eyebrow raised. "Like it or not, you saved my hide, Ginny Huggins. Jus' take the food, will you? Then we can call it even."

"Well," I said slowly, "I do love me some bologna sausage . . ." With a smile, I pulled my quilt out from Thimble's saddlebag, and we went over to a lone tree in the middle of the field. We laid it out in the shade beneath it, and Silvio took out all the food from his bag. I threw in a couple of Ma's puny garden tomatoes that I'd taken with me when I left. Before I could tear into the bread, Silvio waved me away and spent a good ten minutes carefully piling up the meat and cheese and tomatoes into sandwiches that were almost too pretty to eat.

"Where'd you learn to do that?" I asked him.

"My mama," Silvio replied, arranging the bread just so. "Before I left, I told her that one day I'd own my own restaurant, and I'd cook all the special things that she taught me to make. And people there would jus' throw money at me because it was so good. Silvio's Place. That's what I'd call it."

I nodded and took a bite of the sandwich.

"Good?" Silvio asked, his eyes searching my face.

"It's heaven," I groaned, my mouth full of food. "If I had any money, I'd definitely throw it at you."

He laughed.

We ate there under the tree, drinking cool water from our canteens and watching Thimble graze on scrub and tumbleweeds. It was the finest meal I'd had in a long, long time.

Chapter 7
Something Good

"So," Silvio said once we'd finished stuffing ourselves silly with all that good food, "where are you and your horse off to, anyway?"

"California," I answered. "San Joaquin Valley." The words sounded so exotic on my lips. I imagined green fields of grapevines and orange groves as far as the eye could see. After all those years in dusty Oklahoma, a place like that sounded like something out of a fairy tale.

Silvio's eyebrows went up. "Really? Me too!"

"You're jokin'!" I said so loudly that Thimble nearly spooked. "You got family there? My ma got some cousins up that way I'm headin' to see."

Silvio shook his head. "No family," he muttered. "Jus' hopin' to get a job as a picker or somethin' like that. Maybe work in a restaurant washin' more dishes, if I'm lucky."

"Right," I agreed. "I need a job so's I can send money back home to Oklahoma."

"You still got folks there?" Silvio asked.

I nodded. "Ma and Pa and my big sister Gloria. How about you?"

Silvio looked away, his eyes on the horizon. "Got a little sister, Marisol. She and my mama are stayin' with my uncle in Guymon. But Papa—he's gone."

My mouth suddenly went dry. "Gone?" I repeated.

"The dust sickness," Silvio said. "Few months back. That's why I went on the road, so I can take care of Mama and Marisol, and make sure they got everythin' they need. It's what Papa woulda wanted."

"Gosh," I said, "I'm real sorry I asked, Silvio." I'd heard about the sickness that came from breathing in too much of the dust. The last couple of funerals at the church were for people who'd died of it. Not knowing what else to say or do, I picked up a stick and started drawing figures in the dirt.

When I looked up again, Silvio was staring out to the horizon. "S'okay," he said softly. "Please, no te preocupes. I mean, I miss him. Miss him real bad. But I got a big family, and they'll take good care of Mama and Marisol while I'm gone. And, hey, I met you and your fast horse, and we got to eat together under this here tree. So I figure today, I might as well be happy."

I shook my head. "Wish I could think like that," I said. "I been havin' a real hard time bein' happy with things lately."

"No hay mal que por bien no venga," Silvio said, a small smile touching his lips. "It's somethin' my papa always used to tell me. Means that even when everythin' seems bad, somethin' good always comes from it."

"Huh," I said, a sting of pain in my heart. "That sounds a lot like somethin' my pa would say, too." Silvio and I were silent then, both watching the parade of jalopies and trucks roll by on the highway across the field.

"Anyway," Silvio said, standing and shouldering his refilled pack. "It's 'bout time I got some road behind me before it gets too hot."

I stood up, too, shaking the dirt from my quilt before rolling it up again. "You interested in some company?" I asked. "Thimble here's got room for two, don't ya, boy?"

Hearing his name, Thimble looked over and nickered, his mouth full of scrub grass. "See?" I said with a laugh. "He agrees."

Silvio looked surprised. "You sure? I don't wanna trouble you none."

"Wouldn't be no trouble," I assured him. "In fact, I wish you would. The ride would be a lot more fun with someone to talk to."

Silvio beamed. "Well," he said, "you don't have to ask me twice! California, here we come!"

After packing up the saddlebag and checking Thimble's hooves, we climbed up into the saddle— me in front, Silvio in back. Thimble headed toward the highway in an easy jog, warming up his legs for the day's journey. Silvio whistled a jaunty song as we went, and my mind drifted to something he'd said about his trip to California:

It's what my papa woulda wanted.

Was this what *my* pa would have wanted? I wondered. Probably not. I imagined him waking up that morning to find my bed empty, Thimble gone, and the little note I'd left them, waiting on the kitchen table.

Dear Pa, I'd written, *Couldn't let you sell Thimble, but I didn't want to burden the family anymore, either. So we went to find a job out West. I'll send whatever I can back to you, to help keep the farm going. I know how important this land is to our family. Don't worry about me, I got everything I need. Tell Ma and Glo I love them.*

Your girl, Ginny

Would he be mad? Sad? Proud? Maybe all of those things put together?

I squeezed my eyes shut, trying to drive the thoughts from my head. I couldn't worry about

that, not while I had Thimble—and now Silvio—
to think of. We had a long road ahead of us, and
if we succeeded, it would be better for everybody.
You're doin' the right thing! I told myself. *How could
it be wrong, if all these other people are doin' it, too?* I
let the sounds all around me—the rattling of loose
furniture, the crying of babies, and the rumbling
of engines—drown out the nagging doubts in my
mind. When I opened my eyes again, I could barely
hear them at all.

We traveled for a couple of hours, and as the sun
rose in the sky, the crowded highway began to thin
out as people stopped for lunch. We'd just finished
getting Thimble fed and watered at a farmhouse
a couple of miles off the main road when I saw
something strange up ahead. "What's that?" I asked,
pointing at the thin stream of white smoke rising
into the sky.

Silvio shaded his face with his hand and squinted into the distance. "Looks like a broken-down car," he said. He was right. As we got closer, I could see the smoke was coming from the hood of a long black automobile that looked nicer than any other I'd seen. A man in a navy suit was frantically waving the smoke away and trying to get a look at the engine. Another man—a big, tall fellow in white shirtsleeves, tan trousers, and with a fedora on his head, stood by watching, his hands on his hips.

"Not a great place for it, either," Silvio added.

I nodded. We were still a ways off from rejoining the highway, and there wasn't a single other vehicle in sight. I was about to say something else when a coughing fit came over me. After I took a swig from my canteen, I felt much better. When I was finished, I saw Silvio looking at me, his dark eyes searching. "You all right?" he asked.

"Sure I am. Musta swallowed a fly or somethin'."

I turned Thimble toward the smoking car. "C'mon," I said. "Let's go see if we can help."

Silvio snorted. "How are *we* s'posed to help *them* rich-looking folks?" he asked.

I shrugged. "I dunno. But Pa always said we should never turn away from a stranger in need, even if we don't have much to give. It's in the Bible."

"Well, all right," Silvio said. "If your pa and the Bible said so, we'd better do it."

The big man turned to see us approaching the car. He was as tall as a tree, and his clean-shaven face was pink with the heat. "Can I help you, kids?" he asked. From the way he talked, I could tell right away that he wasn't from around here. His voice was clear, and it reminded me of the kind of gentlemen who read out the evening news on the radio.

"Actually," I said, "we were wonderin' if *you* might need a bit of help." I pointed my chin toward the smoking car. "Looks like you're purty good and stuck, mister."

He chuckled and glanced at the other man, who was peering under the hood of the car. "What do you think, Charlie?" he asked.

"Engine's overheated, Mr. Bennett," Charlie replied. "We gotta get someone to check the water pump. Might just be some rust jamming up the works, but this old girl won't start unless we get it fixed."

The big man, Mr. Bennett, sighed and looked back at us, mopping his brow with a white handkerchief. "I guess you're right; we are good and stuck. But what do you kids propose doing about it?"

Silvio and I thought for a spell. "Oh!" Silvio finally said with a snap of his fingers. "We passed a gas station back on the highway. Not too far from here. Bet they could fix your car."

"That's right!" I said, remembering the old Texaco station we'd seen. "Pretty sure Thimble could pull you there." I patted Thimble's neck and thought he stood a little straighter.

Charlie had wandered over from the car to join Mr. Bennett. He was younger than his traveling companion, and his long, narrow face was covered in grease. "You're joking," he said, glancing dubiously at my horse. "That scrawny creature couldn't pull a tractor, let alone a Buick!"

I slid off the saddle and walked right up to that man, my arms crossed over my chest. Virginia Huggins *never* backs down from a challenge, and that sounded a heck of a lot like a challenge to me. "Well, I think he can," I said, with as much courage as I could muster. I turned to Mr. Bennett, who was obviously the boss of the two. "Whaddya say, mister?"

Mr. Bennett rubbed his chin. "We probably could get him hitched up to the front with some of the equipment we've got in the trunk." He looked back at me. "And what do you expect in exchange for your assistance?"

I shrugged. "Lunch?"

"But, chief!" Charlie protested. "This is crazy, that horse pulling the car!"

Mr. Bennett gave the man a long look. "Do you have a better idea?"

Charlie crossed his arms and stared at the car for a while. Finally, he sucked his teeth and said, "I guess I don't, sir."

Mr. Bennett chuckled and reached out a hand that was twice as big as mine. "Well, little lady, that settles it. You've got yourself a deal."

I shook his hand and turned back to Thimble. Silvio was still in the saddle, looking as entertained as if he were in the front row at the cinema. Thimble pawed the ground and blew through his nostrils. He knew his honor was at stake. "You ready, boy?" I said with a grin. "Let's show 'em how it's done."

Chapter 8
The Heart of a Lion

Silvio and I did our best with Mr. Bennett's equipment, and soon we got Thimble hitched up to the front of that black car pretty good. "We're all set," I said to Mr. Bennett. "Silvio and I will ride Thimble—all you got to do is put the car in neutral and steer."

"Whatever you say, Miss . . ." Mr. Bennett looked at me expectantly.

"Virginia Huggins," I replied. "But everyone

calls me Ginny. And this here is my friend Silvio Hernandez."

"Pleasure to meet you both," Mr. Bennett said with a broad smile. "Lead the way, Miss Huggins."

He and Charlie got into the car, and I climbed back into the saddle in front of Silvio. With the noontime sun beating down on us, it was hotter than blazes out there. Just breathing the scalding air made me cough, so I took a good long swig from my canteen before picking up the reins.

"You sure 'bout this?" Silvio asked me.

"Sure I'm sure," I said. "We can't jus' leave those fellas out here to melt. Besides, Thimble's up for it, aren't ya, boy?"

I patted Thimble's neck, and he stood tall, his silvery coat shining under the bright sun. *You know I am!* he seemed to say.

Squeezing Thimble's sides with my heels,

I clicked my tongue and spurred him forward. Thimble began to pull, the muscles in his neck and shoulders bunching up as he strained against the harness. With the car's back tires parked in the dirt, the first pull onto to the road was going to be tough.

Thimble pulled and pulled, but the car wasn't budging. I could see Mr. Bennett's face creased with concern. In the passenger seat, Charlie was shaking his head, probably thinking, *I told you so.*

"C'mon, boy," I whispered into Thimble's ears. "You can do it, I know you can! Why, if you pull us all the way, I'll get you a whole basket of apples. The juiciest ones I can find!"

Behind us, the car moved forward an inch, out of the dirt. "It's working!" Silvio exclaimed.

"And a whole box of sugar cubes!" I continued excitedly.

Thimble lowered his head, straining against the

harness with all his might. The car lurched another foot forward.

"And a bag of those little peppermint candies that you like!" I shouted.

With one last yank, the car popped onto the road and started to roll smoothly along behind us.

Yes!

I could feel Thimble's body relax as the weight on him lifted, and he could trot along like normal. "You did it, boy!" I exclaimed. "That was amazing!"

Thimble whinnied and turned to look at me, his eyes sparkling. I'd never seen him so proud. Keeping a steady pace, we made our way slowly down the road.

Silvio laughed with delight, and I turned back to look at him, my heart blooming with pride. "Piece of cake," I said with a wink.

About twenty minutes later, we pulled into

the little white Texaco station. There were two red pumps out front, with a Coca-Cola sign up on the roof. Standing on the ground beside the door was another sign that read: FISH AND CHICKEN DINNERS. A family in a rust-colored jalopy was filling up their tank when we arrived, and they watched us with curious eyes. A horse and two dusty kids pulling a fancy black automobile. We must have looked a sight!

I dismounted and watched Mr. Bennett and Charlie get out of the car. "Well now," Mr. Bennett began, looking over at his young friend. "Looks to me like you just lost a bet, Charlie."

Charlie dragged a sleeve across his forehead and sighed. "Guess you're right, chief. I just didn't think that horse had it in him."

"Hmph," I grunted, crossing my arms over my chest again. *He's sure got a lot of nerve!*

Mr. Bennett walked over to us and gave Thimble's head a pat. "I must say, Miss Huggins," he said, "I am impressed. It looks like your little horse has got the heart of a lion. His riders, too."

"You got that right," Silvio muttered and elbowed me in the side.

I shrugged, my cheeks hot. "Anybody coulda done it, with a good horse like mine."

"Just because anybody *could*, doesn't mean everybody *would*," Mr. Bennett said. Thimble leaned into Mr. Bennett's hand, which is something he only does to people he likes. I couldn't blame him. I didn't like that Charlie too much, but Mr. Bennett sure was nice. "Now, why don't you two kids come inside and take a load off? You just earned yourselves some lunch."

While Silvio and I got Thimble unhitched and set to graze in the shady field out back, Mr. Bennett and Charlie went to talk to the mechanic about getting the car fixed. Once we were done, we all went into the diner inside the station to see about a meal.

It was a cramped little place, with only four booths and half a dozen red stools at the counter. A radio was playing music while the sounds of sizzling and clattering pans came from the kitchen in the back. Movie posters and framed Hollywood photographs hung on the walls, and it smelled like butter and hot coffee. We sat ourselves in one of the booths and squinted at the menu posted on the wall behind the counter. I should have been starving, but for some reason I had no appetite at all. Even though we were finally out of the hot sun, I still felt too warm. The stress of the ride there must have taken it out of me.

I could feel Silvio staring at me as I tried to figure

out what to get. "What?" I snapped.

"Nothin'," he said, lowering his eyes again.

When the cook came around to ask us what we wanted, Mr. Bennett ordered a round of Coca-Colas. He and Charlie both got hamburgers, while Silvio chose a bacon-and-egg sandwich. When they all turned to me, I swallowed and said, "Can I jus' have some buttered toast, please?"

Mr. Bennett cocked his head. "Don't you worry about the money, Miss Huggins—you get whatever you like."

"That's all I want, thank you," I said. The cook nodded and made his way back to the kitchen. He came back a moment later with four ice-cold bottles of Coca-Cola. I pulled one toward me and took a long drink. It was so cold and sweet and bubbly that it almost instantly made me feel better.

"So tell me," Mr. Bennett said after taking a long

swig of his own soda, "what brings two young people like yourselves out on the road?"

"I'm goin' to California," Silvio replied. "Papa got taken by the dust sickness, so I wanna work and send money back to my family."

"Mighty big of you, Mr. Hernandez," Mr. Bennett said and turned to me. "And how about you?"

After guzzling down more than half the Coca-Cola, I said, "I'm goin' there, too. My pa was gonna sell my horse, on account of us not makin' enough money to keep the farm, but I jus' couldn't let 'im do it. So Thimble and I left Keyes to head west. My ma's got some cousins there, and I can get a job, like Silvio. My family'll be better off without us there, weighing 'em down and all."

Mr. Bennett looked at me curiously. "Your pa told you that, did he? That they'd be better off without you?"

I swallowed the last sip of my drink and glanced out the window. I could see Thimble out there, standing under a tree. He was looking straight at me, and for the first time, I wondered if he missed home. "Well, no, he didn't say that exactly," I finally replied.

"What did he say, Miss Huggins?" Mr. Bennett asked, his voice soft. It was strange, that soft voice, because it came from a man as big as a mountain. He looked even bigger inside that tiny restaurant.

I cast my mind back to the argument I'd had with Pa, on the road coming back from Boise City. "He said he didn't know what to do with me—that I was always makin' things harder. And that he jus' *had* to sell all that stuff. He said they weren't important at all." Just thinking about it got me bothered again. "But those things . . . They're part of our family, too. They got all our memories in 'em. If I got rid of everythin' that made me Virginia Huggins, then what's left?" I nodded toward the empty Coca-Cola bottle. "I'd end up jus' like that. Still standing, maybe, but nothin' on the inside."

Mr. Bennett leaned back in the cramped little booth, crossed his arms over his chest, and sighed. "You know what I think?" he finally said.

"What?" I asked quietly. The last thing I felt like doing was listening to another grown-up lecture me about being an ornery girl with wild ideas, but I didn't want to be rude to Mr. Bennett.

"You and your father . . . I think you're both right," he said.

"You do?" I said in surprise.

"I do."

Well! I didn't expect to hear that. I sat up a little straighter. "I mean, I *know* family's the most important thing," I said, thinking aloud. "It's not like I'd sell off my big sister before my favorite pair of overalls—though sometimes I'd like to. But when things get real bad, like they been, I jus' think that havin' those special things around helps us remember what we're fightin' for, y'know? But Pa . . . he just wouldn't hear of it."

Mr. Bennett stared out the window, watching the cars roll by. "I think that you and your pa probably fight like a couple of cats only because you're so alike. You know how I know?"

"How?"

"Because I have a daughter, too," he said. "Sarah. She's all grown up now. But when she was young, we used to argue about all kinds of things! She was stubborn, that girl, just like her father." He looked back at me. "But let me tell you something, Miss Huggins. No matter how much we fought, and no matter how difficult things got—I never, *ever* thought that I would be better off without her."

I blinked and looked down at the table as tears welled up in my eyes. Luckily, that was the moment when the cook showed up with our plates of food and a couple more Coca-Colas. Soon we all had our mouths too full of food to talk anymore, and that was fine with me.

Half an hour later, after we all finished eating and Mr. Bennett had paid the bill, Silvio and I were out back with Thimble, getting him ready for the road again. I fished a few sticky sugar cubes out from my pocket and offered them to him in my open palm. "Swiped 'em from the table in the diner," I explained. "I know it ain't a basket of apples, but it's the best I can do for now. Once I get that job out West, I'll buy you all kinds of treats.

Okay?" Thimble didn't seem to mind; he just gobbled them up and huffed at my empty hand when they were gone.

I climbed up into the saddle and looked over at Silvio, who was staring at the horizon like his mind was a thousand miles away. He'd been acting real strange ever since we got to the diner. "You ready to go?" I asked.

He blinked and glanced up at me, squinting into the afternoon sun. "Yeah, okay," he said.

I clicked my tongue and led Thimble up to the front of the Texaco station, where Mr. Bennett was standing by the black Buick. "She's good as new," he said, patting the hood. "Thanks very much to you both—for your help and your company. It's always good to meet new people on the road! Now here, I want you kids to have this." He reached into his pocket, pulled something out, and pressed it into my hand. I looked down and gasped.

It was a ten-dollar bill.

"B-but, you already bought us lunch!" I stammered. "This is a lot of cash!"

Mr. Bennett closed my hand over the bill and smiled. "I hope it helps you two on your way. But do me this one favor, Miss Huggins, will you?"

I nodded. "Sure, Mr. Bennett. Anything."

"Go home," he said. "I have a feeling your father is heartsick without you. And the rest of your family, too. I'm sure the problems on your farm are difficult to bear, but better to bear them up together."

I looked away. "I . . . I'm sorry, I can't promise you that, Mr. Bennett. You don't understand—"

"Maybe I don't," he said. "But maybe I do. Just think about it."

Try as I might, I couldn't look Mr. Bennett in the eye. So I looked at the road instead. "Okay," I said, nodding. "I'll think about it."

It wasn't until I watched Mr. Bennett's car disappear into the distance that I realized that after all I'd told him about me and my life, I didn't know a single thing about him.

Chapter 9
Fever Dreams

The hours wore on, each feeling longer than the last. Silvio, Thimble, and I took refuge in an abandoned barn during the hottest part of the afternoon and hit the road again just as the clouds began to redden with the setting sun. Pretty soon, the whole big sky was an explosion of pink, purple, and orange—as colorful as fireworks.

Even though all I'd really done that day was ride, I was completely worn out. More than once, I fell asleep in the saddle. I'd wake up a few seconds later to Silvio holding me by the shoulders, keeping me from tumbling to the ground below. He kept telling me to pull Thimble off the road so we could stop and rest, but I told him no. We'd already lost too much time, and we needed to put more road behind us before the day was done. I'd pushed Mr. Bennett's words way in the back of my mind, and I was determined not to think about anything but how many miles were left until the California border. Thimble kept looking back at me, his eyes asking questions I didn't want to answer.

But when I started up with another coughing fit, Silvio yanked the reins from my hands and steered Thimble off the road. "Hey, whatcha doin'?" I asked between coughs. Silvio didn't answer. Once we were out of traffic, he jumped out of the saddle and led Thimble under a clump of trees where he could graze. Still coughing, I jumped down, too, and took another long drink from my canteen and finally got ahold of myself. "It's fine," I said, my voice raspy. "Prob'ly just breathin' in too much dusty air on the road today. We'll jus' ride for another hour or—"

"It's not fine!" Silvio said, with surprising force. "*You're* not fine! Can't you see that?"

I froze. Silvio had hardly said two words since we left the Texaco station, and suddenly it seemed like hours and hours of pent-up talk was bursting out of him all at once. "Silvio," I said, "I swear, it's jus' a little cough."

Silvio's whole body was shaking, and his face was crinkled up with a terrible sadness. "That's how it starts," he said softly. "With a little cough. Then the fevers come, and the pain. Here." He put his hand on his chest. "And then it gets worse and worse until . . ." Silvio swallowed and closed his eyes.

When he opened them again, they were pleading. "I've seen it with my own eyes, and I don't want to see it happen again to you. Mr. Bennett was right. This journey ain't right for you. I know what it's like to lose someone you love. Don't let yourself be the one who's lost. Not when you still have a home to go to—a *Papa* to go home to. You got to go back, before it's too late."

I stumbled back from the impact of his words. "No," I muttered.

"Ginny, please," Silvio said. "You saved my life. Now let me save yours."

I didn't want to believe what he was saying, but deep down, something was telling me he was right. And just like that, all the doubts about this entire plan came pouring into my mind: how much I missed my family, how scared I was, how terrible I felt, and how worried I was to admit the possibility of one awful, horrible thing:

That maybe, just maybe, I'd made a big mistake.

Silvio and Mr. Bennett were right. I had to go home.

"All right," I said. "I'll go back to Oklahoma."

Silvio sagged with relief. "Gracias a Dios."

"But how 'bout you?" I asked him. "You still have to make it all the way to California."

Silvio shrugged. "I'll figure it out," he said. "Maybe hop another train at the next station or hitchhike my way there."

I didn't like the sound of that. In fact, I had a much better idea. I ran back to the saddlebag and pulled out the diary I had brought and a nub of a pencil. After ripping out a piece of paper, I started to write. When I was finished, I walked back to Silvio and handed it over.

"What's this?" he asked, his dark brows furrowed

at my scribbled handwriting.

"It's the names and address of my ma's cousins in the San Joaquin Valley and a note to them from me, sayin' that you're my very good friend. Maybe they can help you get settled. Maybe even get you a job in a kitchen somewhere, makin' people bologna and cheese sandwiches."

Silvio looked at the paper for a moment, and then back at me. "Thank you," he said with a smile. "Maybe they can."

"I put my own address on there, too. So when you come back to Oklahoma, you can find me and tell me all 'bout your adventures out West. Oh, and one more thing," I said, digging inside my pocket. "I want you to have this." I held out the ten-dollar bill.

Silvio stared at the money in disbelief. "Ginny, c'mon now . . . ," he said. "What about Thimble? I know that money could help keep your pa from sellin' 'im for a while."

The thought had crossed my mind, but I shook my head. "You need it more'n I do," I said, nudging it toward him. "I don't want you ridin' those rails unless you've got a ticket in your pocket. I didn't save your hide just to have it beaten up by another 'bo chaser."

Silvio took the money and then pulled me into a fierce hug. "It's been good knowin' you, Virginia Huggins," he said, his voice muffled. "You're a true friend." When he stepped back, he gave me a little push toward Thimble. "Now, promise me you won't stop to help anyone else on the way. No matter how handsome they are." He winked.

"Oh, all right," I said, rolling my eyes. "I promise."

"Good. Now get back on your fast horse, and go!"

I climbed back onto Thimble's saddle, which felt sort of lonely without Silvio. "Good luck," I called out to him. "Make sure to write!"

Silvio waved as I bent my face close to Thimble's ear and whispered, "Come on, boy. Let's go home."

Thimble must have understood because he gave an excited whinny and took off down the road, right back the way we came.

~

Thimble and I rode on and on, the world growing quiet, empty, and dark all around us. I knew it was still plenty warm out there on the open plain, but I was shivering like a leaf. The coughing fits didn't come often, but every time they did, my chest hurt worse and worse.

I'd lost track of how many miles we had to go. It was hard enough to see road signs out there in the darkness, no less any kind of landmarks I might recognize. We stopped a couple of times so Thimble could get a drink and graze, but other than that, we kept going. I knew I should have been eating and drinking, too, to keep my strength up, but I couldn't bear the sight of food. And my canteen was running on empty.

Pretty soon, just staying awake was hard work. I could see Thimble's muzzle pinched tight, which was something he only did when he was worried. "Oh, stop your fussin'," I said, my voice weak. "I just need a catnap, that's all." But even I didn't think it sounded very convincing.

In fact, I was getting sicker by the minute. I could hardly hold my head up, and even the gentle movement of Thimble's gait was making me dizzy. I pulled a rope from my pack and tied myself to the saddle so that even if I fainted, I would stay put.

More time passed; I don't know how long. At one point, I remember seeing an old abandoned farmhouse—windows all boarded up, the front door hanging off its hinges like a broken tooth. The little garden had once been full of rosebushes, but all that was left were thorny, furious tangles that looked like they didn't even remember the look of a summer bloom.

In my confused state, I imagined it was my own house. That I'd gotten home too late, and everything had been sold off, and my family went and left without me. Somewhere in my mind, I knew it wasn't true. But by then, everything was starting to feel like a dream. "Ma! Pa! Gloria!" I called out. "I'm so sorry I left. Please come back!" But there was no answer.

A huge black bird perched on the rusted-out mailbox by the road. He watched us as we passed with an eye that looked as big as the moon, and when he opened his mouth to caw, the sound was an earthquake that shook the earth beneath me.

"Thimble," I moaned as I fell into a deep hole, darker than dark. The whole world was slipping through my fingers like sand, and I couldn't hold on to it anymore. "Please don't leave me, too . . . Thimble . . ."

I don't remember much of anything after that.

Chapter 10
The Longest Night

A voice pulled me back from the dark place. It was quiet at first, just a whisper in the corner of my mind. The world rocked gently, and I felt heavy, so heavy. I lay with my face pressed against the warm, breathing body beneath me. All I wanted to do was sleep.

But the little voice grew louder and louder, and it was calling my name.

"Ginny!"

I groaned. Everything was starting to come back, though I wished it wouldn't. The thirst, the fear, the pain. My chest felt like it was stuffed full of straw, and I wheezed with every breath.

"Ginny, wake up!"

And then I felt hands untying the rope that held me in the saddle, pulling me down into strong, familiar arms. I opened my eyes to see a man looking down at me, his face in shadow from the pink light of dawn shining at his back. When I finally got a good look at him, I had to wonder if, like Rip Van Winkle, I'd somehow slept for a hundred years, because I never knew my father to look so old.

"Pa?" I croaked. "Is that you? What happened?"

When Pa saw that I was awake, he squeezed his eyes shut and tilted his head up to the sky before looking back at me. "You ran off, Gin—that's what happened. But your horse brought you back," he said, his voice angry, happy, and exhausted all at once.

"I had to go," I said, "so I could stay with Thimble. I was gonna send money to help the family. But then I got kinda sick—" I stopped mid-sentence to cough, a sound that seemed to chill Pa right to the bone. His eyes got real wide, and he hugged me tight to himself and started to run. "Lina!" he shouted as he went. "Ginny's back! Get the doctor here, quick!"

The movement made me dizzy. My head wobbled around, and I managed to see flashes of the little ruined garden and Ma's frightened face; of Gloria, her hair messier than usual; of Thimble trying to follow me, his eyes wild as he was led away into the barn; of my bedroom, just the same as I'd left it two days before. When Pa laid me down on the bed, I thought I'd died and gone to heaven, it was that soft. Had it always been that way? I promised never to take that wonderful bed for granted again.

Everything that came next was a blur. I fell in and out of a restless sleep, where the waking and the dream world were drawn up so close together I couldn't quite tell them apart. But there were some things I remember.

I remember somebody undressing me and pulling a fresh nightgown over my head.

I remember warm, sweet tea, lifted to my mouth one spoonful at a time.

I remember tall Dr. Sturm, with his wire spectacles and his coal-black beard, sitting beside me, listening to my chest with a stethoscope. I remember him standing in the doorway later with Ma, murmuring words that I couldn't make out.

When I woke late that afternoon, finally with a clear head, I found Ma sitting next to me, reading. She wore a gray housedress that made everything about her look colorless. But when I stirred, she brightened and leaned in, putting a hand on my forehead. "Welcome back, sweetheart," she said with a smile. "Thank goodness, your fever's down. You had us all purty worried for a while there."

Her softness confused me. "Ma," I said, touching her hand with my fingers. "Ain't you mad? I ran away, I took food and supplies, and—"

"Oh, I'm mad, Virginia Mae," she replied, her eyes narrowing. "Madder than a wet hen, as a matter of fact." She took a deep breath and sighed. "But I'm more happy than I am mad. 'Cause you came back to us." She squeezed my hand, and I squeezed it back.

I felt like I finally let out a breath I'd been holding for days and days.

I tried to sit up and felt something sticky on my chest underneath my nightgown. I wrinkled my nose. "What is that? And why does it smell so bad?"

"Mustard plaster," Ma said. "Helps with the cough. And I cleaned out the whole place with baking soda and vinegar after you got home. Dr. Sturm said you're lucky to be alive. You got home and out of the dust before it got all the way into your lungs. Another day, and it might have been too late."

I blinked, shocked, and leaned back onto my pillow. Then I closed my eyes and sent up a silent prayer for Silvio Hernandez, the only boy I'd ever met brave enough to tell me I was wrong. His good sense saved my life.

Just then, I heard footsteps in the kitchen, and Ma called out, "Pa! Gloria! She's awake!"

A moment later, the two of them appeared in my doorway. Gloria ran over to my bed and threw her arms around my neck, squeezing me tight. "Gee,

Glo," I wheezed, "it's already hard enough to breathe without you stranglin' me."

Gloria pulled back, her eyes wet with tears. "You scared me, you dumb bunny!" she cried. "I'd smack you if you weren't so sick!"

"I love you, too, sis," I said with a smirk, and Gloria punched me in the shoulder. "Well, you can thank Thimble for getting me home safe—"

Thimble!

I sat up and jumped out of bed like I'd been struck by lightning. How could I have forgotten about my horse? "Pa," I said, dashing over to him, "where's Thimble? Is he all right? I need to see him! Last thing I remember, you were pullin' me off the saddle, and—"

"Whoa, whoa, there," Pa said, grabbing me by the shoulders and leading me back to bed. "You ain't going nowhere right now, young lady."

"But—!"

"No buts. Thimble's home safe—he's out in the barn. I'm lookin' after 'im."

I bit my lip. There was something in the sound of Pa's voice that got me worried. "Tell me he's all right," I demanded.

Pa paused, his eyes flicking toward Ma next to me. Ma looked at the floor.

I couldn't bear waiting another moment. "Pa!" I cried.

Pa sighed. "All right, all right," he said. "There was a rock wedged in his hoof when he got here. I noticed 'im limping and pulled it out right away after we got you inside. It punctured the skin pretty deep. He must have jus' kept on walkin' on it for miles and miles till he got you home. Looks like it might be infected."

My chest got tight, and I could feel tears welling

up in my eyes. Thimble was hurt! If he didn't make it, I'd never forgive myself—

"Now listen," Pa went on, seeing the look on my face. "I cleaned 'im up real good and put a nice bandage on there. He wouldn't eat much, but I gave 'im plenty of water to drink, and he's restin' now. He's a strong horse, and if he makes it through the night, I'm sure he'll be as good as new soon enough."

"Please let me see 'im," I begged. "I'm all right, I promise I am."

Ma and Pa exchanged a look, and Pa nodded. "Okay, Ginny—but only for a minute. You need to stay in bed so you can get your strength back."

The moment the words left his mouth, I was running past him and out the front door of the house, my bare feet slapping against the hard earth as I went.

I found Thimble lying on the floor of the barn,

his silver coat stained red by the sunset light pouring through the open door. He raised his head and gave a weak nicker when he saw it was me. He struggled to get to his feet, but Pa rushed forward to stop him.

"Oh no," I murmured, seeing the bandage swaddling his foreleg and the pile of bloody cloths next to a water bucket nearby. I collapsed by his side, throwing my arms around his neck. "I'm so sorry," I said through a mess of tears. "If I hadn't gone and made you run away with me, you wouldn't be sick at all."

Thimble sighed, and I felt his whole body relax. It was like he was as worried about me as I'd been about him, and now that he saw I was all right, he could finally rest. He pushed his nose against my cheek, rubbing the tears away. *"Come on now, Ginny,"* he seemed to be saying. *"Don't cry."*

But once I'd started, I couldn't stop. Even when

Pa came in to take me back to the house, I just kept on crying.

"It's all my fault," I kept saying as Pa tried to convince me to go to bed. "I should never have left. What good did it do, anyway? You were right, Pa. I'm always making everythin' harder for us."

Pa looked at me, his eyes suddenly serious. "Ginny, I can't tell you how sorry I am that I said that to you. I didn't mean it to be hurtful, even though I know it was. The fact is, sometimes doing the right thing means doing the hard thing. And I'm sure glad that you're here to remind me of that. D'you hear?"

I smiled and nodded. "I hear you, Pa."

"Now, stop that blubberin'," Pa said. "Ain't going to help that horse one bit, having you cryin' your eyes out like that. I'll stay in the barn tonight and keep an eye on 'im, so don't worry. If anything happens, I'll come get you."

But I couldn't go until I'd asked the question that had been running through my mind every minute of our trip home. "Are—are you gonna sell 'im, Pa?" I asked, my breath catching on each word.

Pa sighed and reached a hand out to smooth the hair away from my face. "I can't go and sell the horse that saved my girl's life, can I?" he said. "That horse is family now. Guess he always was."

I gasped with relief. "But what about the farm?"

"We'll figure it out," Pa said, standing up. "If your grandpa and his pa before 'im could make it on this land, so can we. Us Hugginses are made of strong stuff, an' we don't go down without a fight. Somethin' will come along, you'll see. Now go get some rest, Gin. I'll watch over 'im like the moon, I promise."

I went back inside, and curled up in my bed to watch the light fade away through my bedroom window. I kept my eyes locked on the soft yellow glow of Pa's lantern, burning inside the barn until after midnight.

It was the longest night of my life.

Chapter 11
What Courage Brings Home

The next morning, I woke up to Gloria yelling louder than a rooster's crow.

"Ma! Pa!" she hollered. "Come quick! There's a big black car comin' up the road!"

I sat up in bed, thinking of every terrible thing that could have happened while I'd been asleep.

Was that the horse doctor coming? Had Thimble taken a turn for the worse?

Or could it be the police? Could I be in trouble

for saving Silvio on the train?

Or was it the bank, come to repossess the farm? Could Ma and Pa have used up all their savings taking care of me, and now they were flat broke?

I shot out of my room, not even bothering to change out of my white cotton nightgown. "Ginny!" Ma called as I rushed past her in the kitchen, up to her elbows in dish suds. "Where do you think you're goin'?"

I didn't answer but instead threw open the front door and stepped out onto the porch. Gloria stood there, her eyes focused on an automobile pulling up the drive. A car that looked more and more familiar the closer it came.

No, I thought. *It can't be . . .*

But when the black Buick stopped in front of us, and a big man in a suit got out of it, I knew it was true.

"Mr. Bennett," I said, unable to believe my eyes. "What are you doin' here?"

Mr. Bennett pulled the fedora from his bald head and walked toward us with a wide smile. His face was as red as an apple, as if he'd been spending long hours in the sun, though I couldn't imagine why. He looked like a man who spent his days in a tall city building somewhere—not in a cornfield. "Well!" he exclaimed. "If it isn't Miss Virginia Huggins! Lucky for me there's only one Huggins family in Keyes— or else it would have been a real job finding you. I guess you took my advice after all."

I looked down at my bare feet, a little ashamed. "Yessir, you were right. I came home. Just in time, too."

"Smart girl," Mr. Bennett said. "Glad to see you're safe and sound. And who's this?" He gestured toward Gloria.

"Gloria Huggins," my sister replied, primly offering Mr. Bennett her hand. "Ginny's older sister. Pleasure to meet you, sir."

"My, my, what a beautiful family," Mr. Bennett said.

Gloria preened like a peacock. I rolled my eyes.

"But, Mr. Bennett," I said, "I don't understand. Did you really come all this way jus' to make sure I got back home?"

Mr. Bennett turned back to me and winked. "Not exactly," he said.

Around that time, Ma came out of the house, looking flabbergasted to find such a smart-looking fellow on her doorstep. She smoothed down her hair and adjusted her dress, and just like that she was beautiful. I don't know how she does it.

All the commotion also brought Pa out of the barn, blinking into the sunlight like he hadn't slept a wink. Which he probably hadn't.

"Mornin'!" Pa called out to us as he walked up, looking warily at the black car. Charlie had gotten out and was leaning against the trunk, watching us with his arms crossed.

"Oh, don't mind Charlie, Mr. Huggins," Mr. Bennett said with a chuckle. "He isn't exactly warm and fuzzy, but he's not too bad."

Charlie gave a nod, and Pa returned it. "Is there somethin' I can do for you folks?" he asked, looking only slightly less suspicious.

"Actually," Mr. Bennett said, "I was hoping there might be something I could do for *you*. You see, your daughter Ginny and her horse did me a big favor out on the road yesterday. Helped me in a big way. And since I was passing through Keyes on the way up to the Dakotas, I thought I'd stop by and see if I could return the kindness."

"Did she, now?" Pa asked, glancing over at me.

"Their car broke down on the highway, so Thimble pulled 'em to a gas station to get it fixed," I explained.

"That's mighty kind of you, mister," Pa said. "But what exactly are you offerin'?"

Mr. Bennett smiled and clasped his big hands together. "Well, you see, my name is Hugh Hammond Bennett, and I'm the director of the Soil Conservation Service—have you heard of it? My colleagues and I are on a mission from President Roosevelt to help out folks in this region, to get your land growing again."

My jaw dropped. *President Roosevelt?*

We all stood in stunned silence.

"I don't understand," Pa finally managed. "It's not like you can make it rain. How can you help us?"

At that, Mr. Bennett's eyes lit up with excitement.

"I'm so glad you asked. You see, my friends and I have come up with proven new farming techniques that are already helping farmers like you across the nation. If you give me time, I'll give you answers. But not just you—if you get all your friends and neighbors here, I'd be happy to help them all."

Pa looked at Mr. Bennett closely, like he was searching his face for the lie, the con, the cheat inside. He'd already been skinned by those crooked buyers in Boise City, and that hadn't been the first time, either. But this was different. I took Pa's hand into mine and squeezed it. "He's the real thing, Pa," I whispered. "I know it."

That seemed to settle Pa's mind. "Lina," he said, "call up all the neighbors and get 'em over here right away. Glo, get some lemonade goin', would you, please? Enough for a crowd." Excited, Ma and Gloria skittered into the house like two jackrabbits.

"What should I do, Pa?" I asked.

"You come with me," Pa said. He turned to Mr. Bennett. "Excuse me for a second, mister. We'll be right back."

Mr. Bennett nodded and gave me a wink. "Take your time," he said. "I'm sure you two have lots to talk about."

Pa pulled me by the hand toward the barn. As we got closer, my heart started to beat faster. Today was turning out better than I thought it ever could—but what about Thimble?

As soon as Pa opened the barn door, I saw him.

Thimble stood by the window, his silvery coat shining in the sun. Pa must have given him a wash overnight, because I hadn't seen him look so pretty in ages. His black mane and tail were combed and clean, and as soon as he heard the creak of the door, his dark eyes turned to me.

"Oh, Thimble!" I cried. "You're all right!" I dashed over and threw my arms around his neck. He snuffled at my hair and blew his nostrils out, shaking his head.

"Sorry," I muttered through happy tears, "I'm sure I smell downright awful with that mustard plaster all over me. But I'm so glad to see you!"

Pa walked over and gave Thimble a pat on his flank. "I cleaned his hoof again this morning and put on a new bandage. The wound is deep but clean. He'll be limpin' awhile, but I wouldn't be surprised if you were back in the saddle again before the month is out. He's a stubborn beast, jus' like you."

I grinned and covered Thimble's face in kisses. He made a rumbling sound in his throat and nuzzled me back with his warm, velvety nose.

Then I turned to Pa. He was covered in dust— from his boots to his jeans to his bone-tired face. I ran to him and wrapped my arms around his waist. "I'm so sorry, Pa," I burst out. "I'm so sorry I ran away and scared you and made you spend money that we didn't have in the first place jus' to fix up the mess I made."

After a minute, Pa pulled me from him and looked me straight in the eye, his hands on my shoulders. "You wouldn't have run away if I hadn't pushed you," he said. "I should have listened to what you were tryin' to tell me. It's true that we got to make sacrifices to stay on this land, and that's gonna be hard no matter what. But some of the things we keep, even though they're just things—they're *us*. That's right, isn't it?"

I nodded.

"I should never have tried to sell Thimble," he went on. "I see now that he's not a thing to be bought and sold, not to you."

"But what about the money?" I asked. "How are we gonna afford to keep 'im?"

"We'll find another way," Pa said, standing straight and tall, sure as sure. "And maybe your Mr. Bennett will help us out like he says."

I shook my head. "I still can't believe he came all the way here jus' for me! Sent by the president himself!"

Pa smiled. "You see, girl? Your little adventure wasn't a mistake, not really. Courage always brings somethin' home with it."

I felt just as light as a feather, standing there in the barn with so much possibility waiting outside the door. "Oh!" I exclaimed. "That reminds me!" I ran out of the barn and back into the house. In my bedroom, I dropped to my knees beside the bed and scrabbled around underneath it until I found what I'd been looking for.

I found Ma in the kitchen, helping Gloria squeeze lemons and spoon out sugar for the lemonade. I took her hand, still pink from washing, and placed the delicate china teacup in it. The one with the pink roses inside. "Sorry I stole it," I said quietly. "But I couldn't let you give 'em all away."

Ma looked at the teacup for a long time. Then she looked up at me, and ran her hand along the side of my face. "It's good to have you home," she said softly.

I watched her carefully place the teacup back in the glass cupboard. Outside, I could see trucks approaching and hear familiar voices shouting hello—the Atwoods, the Wilsons, and a few of the other neighbors from miles around. Mr. Bennett went out to greet them and shake their hands. The sight of them all together like that made our farm look more alive than it had been in a long time.

I could hardly wait to run to the barn and tell

Thimble the good news! Grabbing up a pitcher of lemonade from the kitchen table and a few glasses, I headed out to the porch to see everyone. I didn't know what was going to happen next, but I sure was excited to find out.

Chapter 12
Indomitable

"Ginny!" Ma's voice called from the house. "Supper!"

From up in the saddle, I saw Thimble's ears flick toward the sound. He knew that supper for me meant supper for him, too, and there ain't nothing my horse loves more than a good meal at the end of a long day. I clicked my tongue and tugged on the reins, and Thimble started moseying out of the cornfields and back toward home.

It had been two months since Mr. Bennett had

come to our farm, and he sure left his mark on the place. Where there'd always been hard, straight lines plowed across the land, his WPA men had helped us make curvy ones instead, with little strips of grass in between each. The men also planted long lines of trees across the fields, which he said would help protect us from the fierce winds of the dusters.

I got Thimble settled out in front of the house with his nosebag of oats and ran inside to wash up. Ma was dishing out plates of chipped beef on toast, with a casserole of baked apples for dessert cooling on the counter. Gloria was busy pouring glasses of milk for each of us, while Pa fiddled with the radio. "Can we listen to some music instead of the news tonight?" I asked as I laid out the napkins.

"Not tonight," Pa replied. "The president is givin' one of his fireside chats in a few minutes—and word around town is that it's about us."

"Oh!" I exclaimed. I loved President Roosevelt's speeches. I didn't always understand exactly what he was talking about, but there was something about his voice that made me feel like I was wrapped up in a big, soft blanket.

"Hey, Gin," Gloria said, pointing her chin toward me. "A letter came for you." She pulled a small, wrinkled envelope from her dress pocket and handed it over. "Looks like it's from California."

"Really?" I asked, grabbing the letter. The return address was written in tiny handwriting to fit onto the envelope. I ripped it open and started to read.

Dear Ginny, it began. *I finally made it to Stockton. I found your nice family, and they gave me a place to stay and hot meals. I asked about you, and they said they'd spoken to your mother on the telephone, and that you are safe and well. Your cousin Ruth has already put in a good word for me at the diner down the street, so I think I will have a job soon. I will remember you and your fast horse in my prayers every night. I hope one day we will meet again.*

—Silvio

Smiling, I folded the letter and slipped it into the pocket of my overalls for safekeeping. I thought about me and Silvio, all grown up, with me going to eat at his restaurant, and him coming to visit me at the farm. My farm. *Yeah,* I thought. *I think we will meet again someday.*

"Who was it from?" Gloria asked, her nose poking in as usual.

"A very good friend," I replied.

Pa was still sitting by the radio, and all of a sudden he started waving his hands. "It's startin'!" he said and turned the volume knob all the way up before joining the rest of us at the table.

"Ladies and gentlemen," the announcer began. "The president of the United States."

There was a pause, and then a familiar voice filled the room. "My friends," President Roosevelt said, "I have been on a journey of husbandry . . ."

I shoveled a few forkfuls of chipped beef and bread in my mouth, but my supper was quickly forgotten as the president went on to talk about the struggling farm families of the "drought states" and the burned-up fields of wheat and corn that he'd seen while he visited there.

"He's talking about us!" Gloria said, nearly upturning her glass of milk.

I was so excited that I wanted to scream! But I was afraid to miss something, so I clapped both hands over my mouth and kept listening.

"Yet I would not have you think for a single

minute that there is permanent disaster in these drought regions," President Roosevelt continued, "or that the picture I saw meant depopulating these areas. No cracked earth, no blistering sun, no burning wind, no grasshoppers, are a permanent match for the indomitable American farmers and stockmen and their wives and children who have carried on through desperate days, and inspire us with their self-reliance, their tenacity and their courage. It was their fathers' task to make homes; it is their task to keep those homes; it is our task to help them with their fight."

We listened for a long while after that, supper getting cold on our plates but none of us wanting to eat. It felt sort of wrong to be gobbling up our toast when the great man was talking. When it was all done, Pa stood up slowly and turned off the radio. We ate our cold food in silence, thinking about everything the president had said.

"What's 'indomitable' mean?" I asked after a few minutes.

Pa looked up, his eyebrows furrowed. I thought he looked very smart in his new flannel, which he bought with the government money he got for working with Mr. Bennett and his men to farm our land in the new way. He got Ma and Gloria new sun hats, too, and a new pair of overalls for me. Even Thimble got a present: a little bag of his favorite peppermint candies. "I don't know exactly," Pa finally said, "but I think it means that nothing can beat us. That no matter what happens, we'll make it in the end."

～

After we washed and dried all the dishes, I went out to settle Thimble in the barn for the night. He nosed at the pocket where I usually kept a couple of sugar cubes, and sure enough, I managed to find one down at the very bottom. Thimble took his time to crunch it carefully, savoring every bit of sweetness he could.

I picked up a curry comb and rubbed it over his shoulders. It was something he always liked before bedtime, and I liked it, too. With how busy everything was these past two months, Thimble and I didn't hardly get a chance to be together except at the end of the day. Things were better since Mr. Bennett had showed up, but things were still hard. We still only had just enough money to get by, it was still hot as blazes, and the dusters still blew in now and again, making a downright mess of everything.

But things were different, too. We had hope. It was just a little bit of hope, but maybe a little bit was all we needed.

"Good night, Thimble," I said, giving him a kiss. "I'll take you across the field again tomorrow, all right? I think it'll be a nice day for a ride."

Outside, the open sky was a quilt of stars, so big that it made me dizzy to look at it. I didn't actually know if tomorrow would be a nice day for a ride. There might be a storm coming, or who knows what. But that didn't matter. Because Thimble and me, and Ma and Pa, and everyone else in Oklahoma—and even Gloria—we were indomitable. The president said so himself.

I rolled the word over my tongue, and it was like tasting something new and exciting.

Indomitable.

Yessir, that's us.

And now, here's a sneak peek at the next

American Horse Tales

Hollywood

by Samantha M. Clark

Juniper gripped the reins tighter as her horse sped across the paddock. Balancing carefully, she pulled her right leg up and over her horse's back. She crouched on the stirrup at his side, and when her target was near, Juniper thrust out her arm.

"Take that, fire breath!" she shouted, brandishing her makeshift sword in the air. "We got it, Able. We got the dragon!"

As the horse sped away, Juniper pushed up onto

Able's back again. She flipped around so she was sitting backward, then grinned at the massive elm tree they had just passed, its crooked branches like clawed arms reaching out to catch them.

Juniper patted her horse's side as he slowed to a trot. "If that really was a dragon, Able, we could've taken it. You and me—we're the best team ever, right?"

She peered over her shoulder as Able neighed, nodding his head as though he agreed wholeheartedly.

Juniper spun around to face forward and said, "Let's go again. This time, let's circle around, like Lady Penelope does on *Castle McAvoy*."

Able's ears twitched as Juniper hunched over his neck, then the horse took off.

"Woo-hoo!" Juniper shouted. "Watch out, all ye drag—"

The rest of her war cry got stuck in her throat. A figure over by the stables caught her eye. It was someone who wasn't supposed to be there. Someone who had said he'd be working in his office for at least the next hour.

Juniper quickly pulled back on Able's reins.

"Abort! Abort!" she said, steering the horse toward the stable. With a nervous laugh, she whispered, "The *real* dragon is watching us now."

Juniper's father shook his head as they trotted toward him.

"What are you still doing in the paddock?" Her father took hold of Able's reins while Juniper slid from her horse's back. "Able's supposed to be cleaned, fed, and resting by now."

"I was going to . . . ," Juniper began, trying to think of an answer that didn't include swords or dragons, but nothing came to her mind.

Her father brushed dust off Able's side. "You can't clean him from the saddle, you know." His eyes dropped to Juniper's waist, then narrowed. "And why is the rasp tucked into your belt?"

Oops! Juniper looked down and yanked the rasp out from where she had secured it tightly between her belt and her jeans. She waved it in the air like she was using it to attack an enemy. "It was my sword?" Each word was filled with uncertainty, as though it wanted to run back into her mouth and hide.

"Wait, don't tell me: A troll is on the grounds, and you just *had* to protect the ranch." Her father's lips loosened like there was a possibility of a smile inside them.

Juniper jumped on the chance to bring it out. "A dragon, actually. Fifteen feet high! No . . . *twenty*! And it was getting ready to burn the whole kingdom—uh, ranch—down, and everything in it.

You, me, Mom, Rose—everyone. Remember what the dragon did in the last episode of *Castle McAvoy*? Able and I couldn't let that happen here. We had to save you guys." She ventured a grin.

"A dragon, huh? In the paddock?"

"A huge one," Juniper said. "The exact size of that tree, in fact." She pointed at the old elm with the claw-like branches.

Her father looked at the tree, then back at Juniper. "So, what you're saying is, if you didn't have to battle a dragon to save our ranch, you would've had Able brushed by now?" He raised one eyebrow, and a giggle bubbled up inside Juniper.

She nodded. "Exactly."

"Okay." Her father whirled around and faced the tree. He stood tall and raised his arms wide.

"Dragon!" her father shouted. "I, King Paul of Ranch Bar K, demand that you halt your threat until . . ." He paused, glancing at Juniper. "Tomorrow afternoon, after school! Be gone until then, oh fiery dragon . . . thing."

He turned to Juniper, slapping his hands together like he'd just finished a job well done.

"There. You can pick up where you left off tomorrow, but *after* you've finished your homework." He smiled. "Deal?"

Juniper bowed low. "Your wish is my command, my king."

"Good, because I need Able happy and healthy tomorrow." He rubbed the horse's nose. "He might have a job."

Juniper's eyes grew wide. "Really? You think he's ready?"

Her father nodded. "He's been doing great with you here at the ranch. And this role sounds perfect for him."

"What it is?" Juniper wiggled her fingers back and forth at her side, excitement building within her.

"It's . . ." Her father held on to his next word, and the suspense bit into Juniper.

"What?" she pressed. Then she saw the twinkle in her father's eye.

"Wait! It isn't . . . Is it . . . Do they want him for . . ." Juniper gulped. "*Castle McAvoy*?"

Her father cracked another smile, and Juniper released all her excitement in a jump and an "AAAAHHHH!"

To be continued . . .